# Ginny remembered the first time they'd met

Across a room, she saw a man suddenly straighten. His head whipped around, and he stared right at her, as if she'd called his name—Bret Calhoun. Then he moved through the crowd toward her. As she watched him approach, it occurred to her that a smart woman would turn and run from such single-minded purpose, but she simply stood, waiting for him.

At last, he stopped before her, holding out his hand. She took it, and he led her onto the dance floor.

"I'm Bret Calhoun," he said at last.

"I know. I asked about you," she admitted.

He tilted his chin up in understanding. "You were interested? That shows promise. Who are you?"

She wasn't sure whether she could trust her voice not to waver, but managed to say, "Ginny McCoy."

He smiled. "Well, the real McCoy. I've found you at last."

Dear Reader,

What an honor for *The Real McCoy* to be the final book in The Bridal Collection.

Those of you who have read *Cats in the Belfry* will recognize Bret Calhoun as the brother of the hero in that book. I found Bret appealing enough to merit his own story, and Ginny McCoy seemed like just the right woman to take him on.

I've always felt that marriage is a journey. The bride and groom begin it by reciting their vows in the presence of their friends and families. After the ceremony, they carry away with them everything they'll need—all the love, hope and faith in each other that will take them through their life together.

In ancient Greece, the newly married couple traveled to the bridegroom's house in a chariot, often accompanied by the bride's father so he could see the place where his daughter would be living. And, at one time in the Scottish Highlands, it was traditional for the bride and her father to be chased on horseback by the groom and his friends. Once she was caught, the bride was "kidnapped" and carried to the church.

While today's weddings may not have that kind of drama, they still have the basic elements that weddings have had for centuries—the commitment of a man and a woman to each other and the best wishes of those who love them. As we head into the twenty-first century, it's good to know that some things never change.

Sincerely,

*Patricia Knoll*

# THE REAL McCOY
## Patricia Knoll

## *Harlequin Books*

TORONTO • NEW YORK • LONDON
AMSTERDAM • PARIS • SYDNEY • HAMBURG
STOCKHOLM • ATHENS • TOKYO • MILAN
MADRID • WARSAW • BUDAPEST • AUCKLAND

This book is dedicated to my parents,
Raymond and Orzola Forsythe, who gave me
my sense of humor and my love of books.

ISBN 0-373-03264-1

Harlequin Romance first edition May 1993

THE REAL McCOY

# PROLOGUE

"COME ON. WE'RE LATE." Ginny McCoy half dragged her father up the steps of the century-old church. At the same time, she urged her younger sister ahead of them by placing a hand on her spine.

"Quit pushing," Carrie complained, turning and glaring at her. "I don't know why you're so wild to attend this wedding. You've had a crush on Sam Calhoun ever since you started playing on his softball team." She spoke with the devastating frankness of a seventeen-year-old. "I wouldn't have thought you'd be so anxious to see him married off." She glanced at Ginny's seafoam-green dress. The gown floated around her sister's petite figure, its handkerchief-point hem dipping to midcalf. Her long hair, as pale as flashes of summer lightning, was permed into waves that drifted around her shoulders. "You should have worn your uniform. Then you and your teammates could stand up when he says 'I do' and weep in unison."

"Oh, be quiet," Ginny answered, giving her sister a sassy grin. "You could have stayed home, you know, but you didn't want to miss the wedding of the year, either."

"Well, I may see some of my friends here," Carrie admitted, stopping before the big double doors to smooth her own short tumble of chestnut curls and pull the neck of her dress away from her perspiring throat. Ginny had told her the pink satin was too warm for the late August afternoon. She would have teased Carrie for not listening to her, but their father, Hugh, spoke up.

"Hush, girls," he hissed as he swung open the heavy oak door of the white frame building. "See, they've already begun."

"Oh, the place is packed," Ginny groaned as they stepped into the wide foyer. Her blue eyes were full of disappointment when she saw that the mahogany pews were overflowing with guests. If it hadn't taken her so long to talk her father into wearing a suit and tie, they would have been on time.

The church was beautifully decorated in shades of coral and mint green. Sam and Laura stood before the altar, and the Reverend Mintnor waited to begin. Conscious of the people turning to stare at them, Ginny searched desperately for a seat.

At last, she saw a space in one of the last pews. It held several of her teammates, who were motioning to her. Grabbing Hugh and Carrie, she hurried forward. They scooted in beside their next-door neighbor, Margie Blaines, who whispered, "Came to see the deed being done, hmm? That Laura Decker is one lucky woman."

"They're both lucky," Ginny whispered back. The guests fell quiet as the soloist stood for her first song.

As the woman's voice soared, Ginny looked around with pleasure. It seemed that the entire population of Webster, South Carolina, was in attendance. This would make quite a write-up for the local weekly paper, the *Herald,* that Hugh owned and edited.

Ginny smiled ruefully as she admitted to herself that Carrie was right. The team members were at the ceremony because they couldn't quite believe the sexiest, most eligible man in town was actually getting married. They'd all had crushes on Sam, even the happily married ones like Margie. As if they had all heard Carrie's words, the pewful of women sighed in communal regret when Sam said, "I do." Carrie giggled and tried to duck away as Ginny elbowed her.

When the congregation stood for the recessional, Ginny strained to see. She loved the romance of weddings and liked to gather ideas for her own future ceremony. She thought a Christmas wedding would be nice, with her attendants in gowns of midnight-blue crushed velvet. Her father would be in a tuxedo and a shirt with pleated front, as would the bridegroom. That was where things always went a bit fuzzy. Not only did she have a hard time picturing her future husband, she couldn't imagine Hugh in a tuxedo.

Ginny grasped the back of the pew in front of her for balance as she stretched onto her toes. She was barely five foot three, and even in high heels, she couldn't peer over the crowd; still, she managed to glimpse the wedding party. She admired Laura's floating white organza gown and the bridesmaids' dresses of bright coral. Sam and his two groomsmen wore formal tuxedos, and she was struck by how much the three men looked alike. She knew Laura's attendants were her sisters and wondered if the two men were Sam's brothers.

As the organ music boomed and the group began its march behind the bride and groom, a prickling of some sixth sense made Ginny aware of the best man, whose head came up just as she noticed him. He gazed straight at her.

He was good-looking, though his appearance wasn't striking. His blond hair, several shades darker than her own, was thick, short and combed back from his face. His nose was straight and unremarkable, his mouth full and firm. But what really drew her attention were his eyes—clear gray, sizzling in their intensity... and focused on her.

Ginny's heart faltered, then bounced into her throat to cut off her breath. Her cheeks heated as blood rushed into her face. She felt conspicuous, certain everyone in the church was watching her stare at him, but she didn't care. Some elemental force held her spellbound and she couldn't tear her eyes away.

He must have felt it, too, because as he walked slowly with the smiling maid of honor clinging to his arm, his attention remained fixed on Ginny. She pivoted in concert with his even stride. She was pulled and held firmly, like the moon caught between the gravity of the earth and the sun. Finally he moved into the church foyer.

As if she'd just been released from the power of an electrical charge, Ginny rocked back onto her heels. It was a moment before her breath returned, but when it did she lifted a dazed face to her father. "Who is that, Dad? The... the best man."

Hugh was busy unknotting his tie and trying to plot the least-crowded path out of the church, so he didn't see her flushed face or hear the catch in her voice. "That's Sam's brother, Bret. I want to meet him. I understand he's a reporter in Memphis. You should try to meet him, too. You'd probably have a lot in common."

"No kidding," she murmured, still shivering from those moments of awareness.

"If you decide not to work for me after your internship, maybe he can give you a line on a job. You should explore all the options."

"Maybe." Ginny followed Hugh and Carrie out of the church as she thought about what had happened—she'd never reacted to a man in such a ridiculous way. She was still trying to recover from it when the three of them arrived at the hall where the reception was being held. By the time they'd congratulated the bride and groom, the dancing had begun. Hugh and Carrie wandered away to get some punch and visit with friends.

Ginny stood at the edge of the dance floor listening to the band and swaying to the catchy rhythm. Her gauzy dress brushed gently against her calves.

Across the room, she saw a man suddenly straighten. His head whipped around and he stared right at her as if she'd called out his name—Bret Calhoun. He'd been flirting and laughing with the bridesmaids, but now his smile faded.

He didn't appear to say a word to the people with him. He simply spun around and moved through the crowd toward her. Ginny's heart took up a drunken lurching cadence as she watched him approach. It occurred to her that a smart woman would turn and run from such single-minded purpose, but she stood waiting as he advanced.

At last he stopped before her, only inches away. His gaze swept over her face, touched on her hair, swung down her body, then came back to her blushing cheeks. She felt as if she and Bret were suspended in time, as if everyone else in the room had melted away, leaving only the two of them.

When the edges of her vision began to blur, she realized she'd forgotten to breathe, and she gasped for air. Hearing the soft sound, he smiled.

And she was lost.

He held out his hand, she took it, and he led her onto the dance floor. They moved to the slow dreamy music as if they'd always been together. Within moments he abandoned traditional hand-in-hand, hand-on-waist dancing. He grasped her wrists and drew them up behind his neck. Then he placed his own clasped fingers at the small of her back.

Her closeness to him was the most astounding yet terrifying experience of her life. There was power and sensuality in him such as she had never known. There was knowledge in his eyes and his touch that far outstripped hers.

He led her out onto a terrace where other couples danced in the dark. Once there he held her slightly away from him and studied her face in the faint light coming from the hall.

"I'm Bret Calhoun," he said at last in a low raspy voice that carried no farther than her ears.

"I know."

"You do?"

"I asked about you," she admitted breathlessly.

He tilted his chin up in understanding. "You were interested? That shows promise. Who are you?"

Her voice could barely be trusted not to waver, but she managed to say, "Ginny McCoy."

He smiled again, one corner of his mouth crooking upward. "Well, the real McCoy. I've found you at last."

She blinked, thinking she had missed a couple of steps in this conversation. "Were you hunting for me?"

"Yes, but I didn't know your name until just now."

"What do you mean?"

Instead of answering, Bret stepped back from her and took both her hands in his, then swung her toward the dying rays of the sun to examine her more carefully.

Ginny knew she was attractive, but she had never been particularly vain. Her looks were merely an in-. heritance from her lovely mother, not something she had achieved on her own. Now, though, she was glad she had flawless creamy skin and pleasing features.

"Are you even a day past eighteen?" he asked, a hint of despair and self-mockery in his tone.

"Of course! I'm almost twenty-three."

He grinned at her vehemence. "You look so young, so untouched."

She shook her head slowly. "That's a strange old-fashioned word to use."

"I think it fits. Are you married?"

"No."

His sigh lifted his chest and the tension holding him seemed to ease. He squeezed her fingers. The pressure was gentle, but she felt it all the way to her bones. "Good. That makes things easier."

"What things?"

"Things between us." He paused, looking at their joined hands, then focused on her face. Ginny had never seen such intensity in anyone. Certainly nothing like it had ever been directed at her. She shivered and her fingers trembled in his. When he spoke again his voice was low as he concentrated only on making her understand him. "I'm not trying to frighten you. I just want you to know that I intend to marry you."

# CHAPTER ONE

GINNY CAME AWAKE slowly and dreamily. She had a
smile on her lips and a sense of bone-deep contentment. She reached out with her left hand and touched
only empty yellow-sprigged sheets.

Her eyes, blue as the South Carolina sky, snapped
open when she encountered the pillow. She was in bed
alone, as she had been every night for the past seven
months. Regret and longing sat heavily on her, but she
forced them down with the same determination she
invoked every morning.

She didn't understand why she missed Bret so much.
Until she'd married him, Ginny had never shared a
bed. After their wedding he'd been gone many nights,
leaving her to sleep alone. And she'd been single again
for several months now....

Unwilling to dwell on the vagaries of a mind not yet
fortified with caffeine, she tossed the covers back,
flung her feet out of bed and stood. She gave herself
a moment to let her emotions calm, then did a few
stretches to unknot her muscles and get her blood
pumping. She knew it would help, too, if she let the
memory run its course, like a reel of film playing to the
end.

She had married Bret Calhoun in a quick courthouse ceremony, barely two weeks after Sam and
Laura's wedding, and left him less than six months

later. Her first anniversary had just passed, unhappily marked by the signing of her divorce papers.

The pain of recalling her marriage sent Ginny prowling restlessly toward the window, her long pink nightgown brushing her feet as she moved. She opened the window and let the cool September breeze sweep into the room.

Rubbing her bare arms, she knelt before the window to peek out at the day. As always after the dream, she felt raw and dejected, unable to understand how she had made such a mistake in choosing someone to love.

As she knelt there, waiting for the tangle of emotions to sort itself out, she had the feeling she was on the brink of a change. All her senses seemed more acute. Scents in the morning air were stronger. The leaves on the maple tree outside her window appeared to have a sharper edge. As clearly as if the woman had been in the room with her, Ginny heard a neighbor call out to her husband, reminding him to pick up a newspaper as he jogged past the convenience store on the corner.

Rising to her feet, Ginny moved her shoulders uncomfortably. Maybe she really was ready to put her marriage behind her and get on with her life.

The strange mood affected her as she brushed her chin-length blond hair back, anchoring it away from her face with a padded satin hairband. Then she dressed in turquoise slacks and a hot-pink blouse because the color combination appealed to her.

Downstairs she began the preparations for breakfast and found herself paying closer attention to actions that had been automatic since she was twelve. While she made toast and scrambled eggs she sipped coffee. Though it was the same brand they'd bought for years, it seemed to taste fresher, more pungent than usual.

She spooned bright red cherry jam into a cut-glass dish, admiring its pure color. Loading everything onto a silver tray, she carried it into the dining room. She and Hugh usually ate in the kitchen, but today she wanted something different.

Her father came down, dressed in old gray slacks and a faded green golf shirt. He was whistling cheerfully as he took his place at the table. When she handed him his loaded plate, he broke off.

"Good morning, honey. Special occasion?"

"Not really. I just wanted to eat in here. We hardly ever have breakfast together, much less a leisurely one." She shifted against the slats of the chair back, but couldn't quite rid herself of the feeling of restlessness.

"Did you sleep okay?" Hugh watched her carefully.

It was obvious that his newspaperman's curiosity was piqued by her evasiveness, Ginny decided. She cursed her expressive face.

"Fine," she chirped, snatching up the morning paper that came each day from Columbia and hiding behind it.

After a few moments of silence Hugh cleared his throat. "Ginny, I have something to tell you."

"Um, what's that, Dad?" Her interest had been caught by an article about the latest round of talks in the Middle East. She'd been considering including an editorial column in the *Herald,* maybe inviting local people to write in, giving their opinions of world events.

"Ginny Kay, listen to me."

When he called her by her whole name things were serious. She lowered the paper. "Yes, Dad?"

"I've decided to retire."

"Retire?" Ginny dropped the paper and stared across the table. Hugh grabbed the coffee carafe to pour himself another cup. He avoided her eyes. "What do you mean, retire?"

"Well, if you want the dictionary definition it means 'to withdraw from business.'"

"I want to know *your* definition." She waited, her face set, while dread spiraled through her. It seemed she was about to find out the reason for her strangely anxious mood. "Dad?" she prompted when he remained silent. "Your definition?"

Her father shrugged as he added cream to his coffee. "I guess it means the same thing to me, too. I plan to withdraw from the business of newspaper publication."

"You're going to sell the *Herald?*" She nearly choked on the question.

"Well, no. I'm going to hire a new managing editor."

If her father had announced he was going to elope with a fan dancer, Ginny couldn't have been more stunned. She opened and closed her mouth a couple of times while heat washed in and out of her face. Her normally pleasant features became a mask of horrified denial. "Hire an..." She gulped. "But, Dad, *I'm* the editor."

He waggled a finger at her. "Acting editor, honey. You know our agreement was for you to do the job until I got over that damned bout of pneumonia, then you'd go back to reporting."

Panic, and a sense of failure, twisted her insides. "That's not necessary. I can—"

He held up his hand. "Let me finish." Once he had her complete attention he took a swallow of coffee and set his cup down. Ginny noticed it rattled a bit against the china saucer. "The truth is, Ginny girl, I've been feeling pretty good for a while. Oh, I've got a ways to go yet, but I'm better. And I've decided it's time for me to retire from the paper."

"Dad, you're only fifty-five," she protested. Her brain was coming out of its state of shock and beginning to whir with questions. "Why would you want to retire so young?"

He grimaced and ran a hand over his thick gray-flecked hair. There was more gray in his hair than there'd been a year ago and certainly more lines in his thin intelligent face. "Because I *am* young. Being sick made me realize that I want to do more with my life than publish a paper."

"Like what?"

"Like write a novel."

Ginny shook her head slowly as she splayed a hand over her chest. "I never knew you wanted to write a novel."

He reached for a piece of toast. "Well, I do. Got a great idea—just haven't had the time to work on it what with being responsible for the paper and raising you and Carrie and all."

Ginny took a sip of her own coffee. She needed a jolt to get her heart moving again. "So, Carrie and I are grown now. She's off to college, I've got my career." She tried to control her panic. "You go right ahead and do whatever you want to do. There's no need for you to hire a managing editor. I can keep on the way I have been since February." Her lips wavered into a bright smile.

Hugh crossed his arms over his chest and set his jaw. "No."

The word lay between them like a ten-pound brick.

Watching him, Ginny couldn't think of another time in her life when she'd seen her father this determined. Usually the most easygoing of men, he now had an expression in his eyes that would have stopped a charging buffalo. Ginny knew she should take the look for the warning it was, but it seemed so out of character she merely sat forward, rested her palms on the thick damask tablecloth and settled in for an argument. "Dad, you've said yourself that I've done a fine job at the paper."

He *had* said that, but it wasn't strictly true, and she knew it. Hugh had been trying to reassure her. Since she'd taken over as managing editor, the paper had experienced every problem from cost overruns to self-destructive printing presses. But she had tried so *hard*.

"You have," he agreed. His voice went a bit reedy and he cleared his throat again. "But you don't have to do it anymore. You don't *need* to do it anymore."

They both knew what he was talking about. When she had come home seven months ago she had desperately needed the challenge of the newspaper to give her focus and purpose. It had been vital that she have something to take her mind off the fact that at the age of twenty-three she was a failure at marriage.

"But, Dad, I want to go on with what I've been doing," she appealed. If she just had a little more time she knew she could have everything running smoothly.

"Don't bat those eyelashes at me, girl. That quit working on me years ago." A smile glimmered on his lips. "Well, okay, maybe days ago. Nevertheless my mind is made up." He leaned toward her, resting his forearms on the tabletop so that he could look into her face. "Don't you see that I've cheated you? And I'm trying to make up for it?"

Dumbfounded, she stared at him. "Cheated me? How could you possibly have done that?"

"By depending on you too much. When your mother died you were only twelve. Carrie was seven." His mouth tightened with remembered pain. "It's not my proudest memory that I acted as if I was the only one in the family affected by Nancy's death. You girls lost your mother *and* your father. By the time I came out of my depression—" he flushed with shame "—and my drunken stupor, you were doing everything from cooking to washing to writing notes to Carrie's teacher. It was easy to let you keep on running the household through your high-school years, and in a way, you seemed to thrive on that kind of responsibility. I even let you put off going to college till Carrie was in high school, but it wasn't right."

"I didn't mind, Dad. I liked being busy."

"That's just the point. You were busy doing *my* job. You should have been out having fun."

"I had fun." She sighed and shook her head in puzzlement. "Daddy, why are you feeling guilty about my adolescence all of a sudden?"

"Because I've done the same damn thing again. Throughout the spring and summer I've had you running the *Herald,* doing all the editorial duties, paying bills, hiring staff, when what you really wanted to do was be a reporter. It's been too much for you. You're hardly ever home before seven, you've lost at least ten pounds you couldn't afford to lose, and I don't think you've been out with your friends since you moved back home."

"There were other reasons I lost weight and . . . and I haven't really wanted to see my friends." Ginny lifted her hands helplessly. "Besides, I knew you needed me."

"I still do, but there's no reason for you to do everything. I've hired a managing editor. You can go back to reporting, which was always your goal, wasn't it?"

"Well, yes."

"That's settled then." Hugh sighed in satisfaction. Suddenly his breath erupted into a cough that rattled and wheezed in his chest.

Alarmed, Ginny bolted from her chair and reached for him. "Dad, are you all right?"

"Fine, fine," he insisted, taking a sip of coffee to ease his throat.

Watching him bring himself under control, Ginny sank back into her chair uneasily and lifted a hand to her mouth. She began nibbling on a fingernail. He seemed to have the whole matter of his retirement settled while she was still reeling. She'd always been able to cajole him into whatever she wanted, but she knew better than to try this time. He'd made up his mind; she could tell.

She had to admit that what he said was true. Running the newspaper had been harder than she'd ever imagined. She often collapsed into bed at night wondering how her father, grandfather and great-grandfather had managed in the days of crank presses and typesetting by hand. It rankled her that even with computers and her years of education, she hadn't done as good a job as the men in her family. She had frequently longed for the straightforwardness of reporting as she'd experienced it during her internship at the big daily in Memphis. With the ease of several months' practice, her mind automatically veered away from thoughts of Memphis before other memories surfaced.

"You aren't going to fight me on this, are you, Ginny?" Hugh asked. "You do see it's for the best? Just think how much easier things will be for you— and for me. I'll be able to get started on my book."

"Well, I don't—"

She was interrupted by another mighty, sustained cough from her father. He bent over until his chest bounced against the table, sending the silver into a rattling dance. "Now, don't argue," he choked out. "It's better this way."

"Yes, yes, of course, Dad. If that's what you want to do," she hastily agreed, once again coming to her feet. "Dad, should I call Dr. Clay?"

Hugh waved her away. "No. I'm fine." He wiped cough-induced tears on a napkin, then dabbed his mouth. "The new editor starts Monday."

Ginny's hand slipped off the armrest as she collapsed back into her chair, resulting in a sharp blow to her elbow. "Ow!" She rubbed it vigorously. "In two days?"

"The sooner the better," Hugh said. His voice seemed to be regaining strength. "This book idea has been rattling around in my head for years. I want to get things arranged so I can concentrate on it. You don't mind, do you?"

A hysterical giggle burbled in her throat. She pushed her fingers through her hair, dislodging her hairband and sending it bouncing onto the gleaming hardwood floor. "No. Heavens, no! Why should I mind that you're changing my whole life in two days' time?"

Hugh gave her a happy smile. "I'm glad you see it that way, honey." He began slathering his toast with cherry jam.

Ginny stared at him for several seconds, then her eyes narrowed suspiciously. She had never known her father to be so set on anything, or so unresponsive to what she wanted. He'd *always* consulted her before making a decision. "Just who is it you've hired, Dad? Anyone I know?"

She could have sworn guilt crossed his face before he lifted the toast and bit into it. With his mouth full, he muttered something that sounded like "Breff Cla-loo."

Dread touched her again and shot up her spine like an electric shock. "What? What did you say?"

Her father took a frustratingly long time chewing and swallowing before he answered. Even then he didn't meet her eyes. "Bret Calhoun," he said.

# CHAPTER TWO

THE ELECTRIC SHOCK became a hot poker spearing her heart. "Bret? You're kidding! Not Bret!" Even as she said the name, she felt a hopeless, helpless flicker of joy. She thrust it aside. "Dad, why on earth would you hire my ex-husband to work on the *Herald?*"

"Best person for the job."

"He's an investigative reporter, not an editor!"

"Now, honey, he's decided on a career change."

"In a pig's eye."

Hugh was beginning to look like a man being hunted by a pack of bloodhounds. "Bret applied for the job, and since he was the most qualified I hired him."

Ginny's shock and confusion hardened to icy anger. Her spine was as straight as a board, her face rigid. "I find that hard to believe."

"It's true." Hugh coughed into his fist. "He's decided to get out of the big city, find a slower pace of life, be closer to his family. His mother lives in Virginia, you know, and Sam lives here. And...and Laura is expecting a baby in a couple of months." Hugh gulped down a mouthful of coffee. He gave her a look that seemed to beg her to understand.

Ginny gaped at him, then laughed in a high, breathlessly wild manner. "Dad, somebody's pulling your leg. Bret loves his family, but he would never leave Memphis unless it was to move to a bigger and better paper.''

''You're wrong there, Ginny girl. He wants to move here. Wants to take life a little easier.''

''That'll be the day.'' She shook her head, trying to clear the confusion. ''Let me get this straight. We're talking about my ex-husband—six feet tall, blond hair, gray eyes.'' Quick wit and even quicker lips, she added to herself with a sigh.

''That's the one. He's a fine newspaperman.''

''Maybe, but he wasn't much of a husband.''

''How would you know? You only gave him a six-month trial.''

Hurt almost doubled her over. She lifted her hands to her throat in an attempt to check the frenzied beating of her heart. ''Dad, I thought you understood.''

He winced and reached across the table to give her an awkward pat. ''I do, honey. I'm sorry. I shouldn't have said that. I'm only trying to make you understand why I hired him. He's the best man for the job and he *wants* the job.''

Her emotions swung again from hysteria to anger. She glared at her father. If someone had touched her with a wet finger at that moment she was sure she would have let off steam. ''Well, he can just take life a little easier someplace else.'' A sudden thought had her turning anxious eyes to her father. ''He hasn't been sick, has he?''

''No, why?''

She shrugged. ''Just wondered why he'd want to move to rural South Carolina unless it was to recuperate or something.''

''He wants to be near family,'' Hugh repeated.

"Then he can get a job working for his brother at the kennel. I refuse to work with him." Ginny dipped a spoon into the jam and aimed a rich mound at her toast.

"Why?" Hugh straightened as if some great new argument had occurred to him. "It's not like you care about him anymore, is it?"

That stopped her cold. She lifted her chin. "Of course not." To prove how unaffected she was, she took a careful bite of toast.

"A person can't hurt you unless you're emotionally involved with him, right?"

For a moment she thought she saw slyness on her father's face, but now he seemed guileless. "Uh, no, but—"

"And you said when you came home last winter that you'd never really loved Brct. It was nothing but infatuation."

"That's right."

"He swept you off your feet. You weren't ready for marriage."

"Now, Dad—"

He held up his hands. "Hey, I'm only quoting all the things you told me. Have I misquoted you?"

Ginny pursed her lips. She was beginning to realize why her father had gained a reputation as a merciless interviewer. "Well, no," she admitted. "But that doesn't mean I want to work with him now."

Her father's angular face took on a long-suffering expression. "I thought you'd grown up in the past few months."

"I have!"

"I thought you'd learned a lot and could maintain a professional relationship with a fellow worker even if he is your ex-husband."

"I can!"

The look of crafty anticipation on Hugh's face reminded her of a cat moving in on a dish of cream. "Good. Then this argument is at an end, and I won't have to interview applicants all over again."

She slapped the uneaten toast onto her plate. "It certainly seems funny that I never knew anything about all these applicants for my job."

"Didn't want to bother you," he said gruffly, then shifted the subject. "You won't quit if you have to work with Bret, will you?"

"Be run off my own family's paper? Never!"

"Good. Good."

Ginny felt as if she'd been neatly maneuvered into a box, then had the lid nailed shut over her head. Dizzily she pressed her fingers to her temples. "Dad, I don't understand why you've done this."

"Because if I learned one thing while I was sick, it's that life is too short to waste. I've enjoyed my years at the *Herald,* but I want out of the newspaper game. I have to confess I never loved it as much as my father did—as much as you do."

The sincerity in his voice had her studying his face. "I didn't know that."

Hugh cleared his throat yet again. "It doesn't matter now. I'm going to start my book, and I know the *Herald* is in good hands."

"But why does it have to be Bret Calhoun's hands?" she moaned, dropping her forehead into her palm and closing her eyes.

"Best man for the job," he insisted again after a long moment of silence, then began to cough.

Panicked, Ginny looked up to see that his complexion was bright red. She leapt to her feet and rushed around the table. Her hands fluttered uselessly over him until he batted them away. "I'm all right," he wheezed. He struggled to stand, his wiry body swaying for a moment as he caught his breath.

"Dad, I really think I ought to call Dr. Clay. You were doing so much better. You haven't coughed like this in weeks. I'm afraid you're having a relapse."

"Don...don't be ridiculous," he sputtered. "I don't want you calling John Clay. He's a fussy old woman who'll make me take vitamins or some such nonsense."

"He's a good doctor."

"Yeah, I know, but all I need is a little fresh air." He raised a fist to tap his chest. "I've got a fishing date with Dave Mintnor. We're going over to Webster Lake to try to catch that albino catfish he saw a couple of weeks ago."

Ginny clapped her hands onto her hips. "Fishing? Are you crazy? You can hardly breathe!"

He straightened the collar of his pale green golf shirt which had become rumpled when Ginny had tried to check his pulse. "I'll be fine. Just fine."

Ginny shook her head in frustration as he headed for the door. "Well, I'm glad Dave is a minister because he may need to pray for divine healing!" Her father merely nodded and disappeared into the kitchen. She could hear him, still breathing loudly, as he rummaged for his fishing tackle in the utility room. Finally the screen door slammed, and she was left alone in the house.

Dazed, she stared at the uneaten remains of breakfast. Had it only been thirty minutes ago that they'd sat down together to enjoy a leisurely Saturday-morning meal?

In that short span of time her life had been picked up, shaken and flipped upside down—again.

Ginny wandered to the window to watch her father drive away. She saw him talking to Jimmy Blaines, Margie's ten-year-old son. Hugh was leaning forward until his face was almost level with Jimmy's. Both of them were gesturing wildly, then Jimmy pointed toward the window. She drew back so Hugh wouldn't think she was spying, but she still stood there, fascinated by their argument. At last Hugh shrugged and reached a hand into his pocket. He brought out some change that he dropped into Jimmy's palm. With a happy wave Jimmy headed for home while Hugh got into his old pickup truck and drove off. Ginny wondered if her father had been negotiating with the enterprising boy for some fishing worms.

Her mouth quirked into a rueful smile. Her father! He'd dropped a bombshell on her, then cheerfully bought some bait and gone fishing! She lifted her hands in helpless wonderment and let them fall back to her sides. At least he was satisfied with his decision, even if she wasn't.

She leaned against the maple sideboard her mother had bought and refinished when Ginny was ten. From here she could look out and see the neighbors beginning their weekend ritual of yard work and car washing.

Why had Hugh hired Bret? She suspected that her father had an ulterior motive, but she couldn't believe he was trying to get her and Bret back together.

He'd been adamantly opposed to their marriage—not because he thought Ginny was too young, but because the whole thing had happened too fast. Also, he knew how disillusioned and devastated she'd been when she'd left Bret.

Ginny turned away from the window. No, her father wouldn't deliberately hurt her; he knew her marriage had been a short and painful mistake.

Of course, there was no way she could have known that Bret Calhoun wasn't ready for a wife. How could she possibly have suspected that he loved his job more than anything or anyone else? That because of his job she would spend most evenings and many nights alone?

So, why was Bret coming to Webster to work for a small-town paper? She couldn't begin to speculate.

Ginny pressed her palms to her knotted stomach and began to analyze her feelings. Her predominant emotion was hurt. She was upset that she'd failed as editor of the *Herald*. She had tried her best, but the problems had been greater than her abilities. And now to have Bret take over after he'd already watched her fail at their marriage...well, she couldn't bear to think about it.

Strangely, she also felt a sense of relief at the thought that someone else would be responsible for the paper. If only it wasn't Bret.

She considered that for a few minutes, idly chewing her lip. Then she straightened. This was a challenge, and she'd never backed down from a challenge in her life. Even though he was her ex-husband and about to take over her job, that didn't mean she had to run and hide.

She was no longer the infatuated girl he had married. She had run the paper by herself for several months while caring for her sick father. She was a professional journalist, from the quality of her work to the correctness of her clothing.

Making a sudden decision, she hurried through the kitchen, snatched up her purse and headed out to do what she knew any sensible woman would do when faced with the certainty of meeting her ex-husband— she would have her hair done, then buy a great new outfit.

ON MONDAY MORNING, Ginny stepped from her car. Her appearance was that of a perfectly dressed professional. She wore a red-and-white jacket with a slim white skirt and teetered slightly on the three-inch heels of matching spectator pumps. After closing the car door, she ran a smoothing hand over her newly trimmed bob. She had chosen the outfit on her Saturday shopping trip because she thought it made her look mature. The jacket may not have been the best choice, considering the heat and humidity of the September morning, but she was a firm believer in the old adage Start As You Mean To Go. It was vitally important she begin this day looking and feeling utterly competent.

Satisfied with her appearance and steadied by a deep breath, Ginny walked toward the front of the brick building that had housed the Webster newspaper for the past eighty years.

A part of her was still upset with her father, who had ducked her all weekend by leaving the house early and staying late at whatever lake or pond was farthest away from her and her questions. If she didn't know how seriously ill he'd been just a few months ago and how precarious his health still was, she would have resented his taking off fishing at a moment's notice. He did need time to relax and recuperate, though.

But she didn't have the slightest doubt he was using her love for him to get her to go along with his plans for the newspaper—and his hiring Bret.

The thought of meeting Bret made her insides lurch sickeningly, but she was determined to brazen it through.

"Start as you mean to go, Ginny," she muttered. She hitched her skirt above her knees and skimmed up the stairs, her petite figure resembling a scarlet cyclone as she rushed in the glass-fronted door of the office.

The place was a second home to her. The outer office had been decorated in dark-paneled wood thirty years before and never updated. The gold carpet was nearly as old as she was, but still serviceable. A waist-high counter ran half the length of the room, and the receptionist, Doris Beekman, sat behind it. She was always the first person in on Monday mornings, which was when she opened the weekend mail and made coffee.

A pegboard hung on the wall behind Doris. Each staff member had a colored peg, similar to a golf tee, that they moved from the "out" column under their name to the "in" column when they entered the office. Ginny's quick glance told her that Doris was the only one in—with the probable exception of Bret Calhoun.

She hurried up to the receptionist's desk, slightly out of breath. "Where is he?" she asked as she rocked to a stop before Doris, who had sat at the very same desk and performed the very same job for twenty years.

Doris's head of frothy red curls came up from the pile of mail she was opening. Slowly she pulled her half glasses down and peered at Ginny over their tops. "Good morning to you, too, Ginny, my dear. My weekend was just fine, thank you."

Ginny winced at the mild reprimand even as she leaned forward to wrap her fingers around the edge of the desk. "I'm sorry, Doris, but you know I'm worried about this."

Doris looked meaningfully at Ginny's bitten fingernails. "I never would have guessed," she said dryly.

Guiltily Ginny curled her fingertips into her palm, mentally kicking herself for forgetting the bet she'd made with Doris that she could stop biting her nails. Whenever she broke her vow, she had to pay up. Sighing theatrically, she dug in her purse and handed the receptionist a dollar.

Doris accepted the bill with a quirky smile and tucked it into a small metal box inside her desk drawer. Eyeing the contents, she asked, "Do you have any idea how much money I've collected from you?"

"Twenty dollars," Ginny answered glumly.

"Twenty-six." Doris closed the drawer with an efficient snap and rested her folded hands on top of the stack of mail.

"Well, I've got a good reason this time," Ginny defended herself. "This is all happening so suddenly, and it's so..."

"Overwhelming," the receptionist supplied sympathetically.

Ginny nodded, grateful that, for a moment, she could let down her guard of bustling professionalism and speak to someone woman-to-woman. She'd always found it easy to confide in the receptionist. In fact, Doris had been like a second mother to Ginny. It was on her shoulder that Ginny had cried when her marriage broke up. And on Saturday, after talking to a sympathetic Carrie, Ginny had called Doris to tell her of Hugh's retirement. The other staff members would be told at a meeting this morning.

Ginny picked at a loose thread on her purse strap, then laced her fingers together. "Have you seen him?" Nervously she reached into a cardboard box on Doris's desk and sifted through a few candid photos. The newspaper usually made prints of all pictures taken at city or county functions, whether they were used in the paper or not. Citizens were welcome to come in and pick up copies.

"Yes, we've already had quite a talk." The letter opener flashed in her hand as she applied it to a stack of window envelopes that contained yet more bills. They were sent by suppliers of everything from paper and ink to utilities, and they always seemed to arrive at the same time.

Ginny gave the pile a despairing glance, wondering how she'd manage to pay them, then brought herself up short as she remembered, with a flutter of gratitude, that it was no longer her problem. She lifted her hands in frustration. "Well? What did you talk about?"

"About the paper, of course."

"What did he say?"

Doris gave her a patient stare. "You can ask him that. I'm not your spy. You can judge for yourself."

Deflated, Ginny said, "I've already judged him."

"That was then, this is now, and things have changed." When Ginny didn't respond, she added, "Everybody'll know that working for Bret will be a bigger change for you than for anybody else."

"No kidding." She pushed away from the desk. Doris was repeating almost exactly what Carrie had said during their Saturday phone call. The two of them had a better perspective on this than she did. "I guess I might as well get it over with. I suppose he's in the boardroom." Not waiting for an answer, she turned on her too-high heels with military precision and started down the hall, deciding to stop in her office and put her purse away before going in search of Bret. The big hobo bag didn't go with the image she was trying to project. Besides, he'd always teased her about it, saying it contained more goods than some major countries exported in a year. Of course, that was one of his silly exaggerations; everything in her purse was essential. Ginny folded the strap, preparing to tuck the purse into the drawer of her desk.

Before she reached her office, though, she passed the open door of the publisher's office, seldom used since her father's illness. She automatically glanced inside.

Surprised, she swung around and stumbled to a stop when she spied Bret sitting in her father's chair. It was swiveled to face the window and his feet were on the ledge. He was tilted far back, gazing indolently outside.

Ginny stared, blinked, then stared again. In the five months they'd worked on the same newspaper—he as star investigative reporter, she as raw intern—she'd never known him to relax. Every moment had been spent writing a story or following leads.

But now he appeared perfectly content to let time pass in unproductive leisure.

Even more surprising were his clothes. In Memphis, he'd owned a fabulously expensive wardrobe of tailored suits and handmade shoes. Now his sockless feet were tucked into long narrow loafers. His baggy stone-washed jeans had frayed hems, and the sleeves of his white dress shirt were rolled up. He wore no tie.

As she gazed at him Ginny had trouble catching her breath. All sorts of emotions threatened to overwhelm her—regret, longing and anger uppermost. She thought she'd buried all those feelings for Bret, but at the sight of him they resurfaced and wrapped themselves around her heart.

He didn't know she was there, and Ginny was grateful to have a moment to observe him. The last time she'd seen him had been seven months ago when he'd arrived at her father's house demanding to know why she'd left. Her stumbling explanations had been met with scorn, then he'd left after telling her he'd never suspected she was a coward.

The memory made her wince, and she lifted her gaze.

With a jolt she realized the glass in the window was reflecting both of them, which meant that he'd been watching *her* watching him.

He turned then, and his gray eyes were as direct and intense as ever. She was sure there was nothing they didn't see. Did he notice the way her heart was battering against the top button of her jacket? See the line of perspiration that had just popped out on her upper lip? Feel the heat that rushed through her?

Ginny controlled her thoughts. Of course he couldn't. He was staring at her thunderstruck face. In a flash, she smoothed her features, stepped into the doorway and greeted him, congratulating herself on the steadiness of her voice. "Hello, Bret."

To her surprise, his piercing eyes took on a positively wicked glint of humor. "Hello, Ginny." He got to his feet with boneless grace, then ambled toward her. "I've been waiting for you."

The way he spoke made her tremble inside, but she held herself still so her reaction wouldn't show. Calmly she laced her fingers together and rested them on the corner of her shoulder bag. "I'm not late," she said.

"Aren't you?" His tone gave the words a deeper meaning she didn't want to explore, so she waited.

He stood in an easy stance as if inviting her to take her best shot. Tension, and awareness of their unique situation, hummed in the air between them like the keening of locusts in lush summer woods.

He looked different, she decided. More relaxed...and happy. Perversely she felt a little quirk of resentment.

Summoning her best social smile, she spoke stiffly. "You look well."

"You look like a million dollars." His own smile was rueful. "Sorry. I know a journalist should be able to think of something more original than that."

It didn't matter. The trite old phrase almost robbed her of speech. "Th-thank you."

"Can't say I'm crazy about the haircut, though. I liked it long."

This was an old argument. One she could deal with. "You didn't have to wash and dry it."

"I offered."

Yes, he had. The memory of his hands in her hair made her scalp tingle. She shot him a quelling glare.

"That's ancient history." Casting about for something to establish a professional atmosphere, she said, "I was surprised to see you relaxing on the job."

"Hey, didn't your dad tell you I came here to take life easier?"

She gave that statement the skeptical look it deserved. "I'll believe it when I see it. Besides, around here we work with our feet on the floor, not on the window ledge."

His shoulders shifted in an effortless shrug. "Well, *I'm* the editor, so I can do pretty much what I darn well please."

That stung. She couldn't hide her flash of pain. However, it quickly gave way to pride. "Does that include moving into my father's office?"

"Yes, it does." Bret twisted at the waist and lifted his hand in a slow sweep of the room. Although he hadn't yet brought in anything of his own, Ginny had the crazy feeling that he'd already put his indelible mark on the place. "Hugh gave me free rein to do whatever's necessary to get the *Herald* back on track," Bret continued. "I'm to turn it into a money-making business, as well as a strong voice in the community."

Ginny dropped her chin to her chest and let her hair cover her face as she attempted to conceal the fresh hurt brought on by that statement.

She had done her best to accomplish those two very goals in the past months, but she knew she'd failed. So did her father and the bankers who had loaned money to the paper. In truth, almost everyone in Webster knew of her failure. What really galled Ginny was that they all chalked it up to her being a woman. Not the fact that she was inexperienced in administering *any* business, much less a newspaper.

Her fists clenched around the fine-grained leather of her bag. She could have done it—given a little more time.

She was startled when Bret reached over and peeled one of her hands away. Although she tried to tug it back he held on firmly. "Nobody expected you to be perfect at running this paper, Ginny." He seemed full of sympathy.

To her horror, tears welled up in her eyes. Quickly she turned her head. "I did what I could."

"I'm sure you did." He sighed, dropping her hand. "Why don't you just show me around?"

She nodded, asked him to wait for a moment, then hustled down the hall to her own office, where she put her purse into the bottom drawer of her desk. Her office had been used by various editors over the years and held mementos of events that had occurred decades before her birth. Framed headlines of long-ago natural disasters hung beside commemorations of visiting VIPs. There was even one minor member of European royalty pictured on a visit during the Roaring Twenties.

Ginny's wooden desk was an old scarred affair that looked as if it had survived a direct hit in World War I. It was completely at odds with the ultramodern computer terminal sitting on its top. Straightening, she checked her appearance in a small mirror she'd hung by the window and saw that she was still presentable in spite of the shocks she'd received that morning. Startled, she saw Bret standing in the doorway. She would have taken a moment to draw a deep breath and run a hand over her fluttering stomach if he hadn't been watching her with such intense scrutiny.

She caught a glimpse of what she thought was yearning in his face, but it quickly disappeared behind a polite smile. Ginny decided she was indulging her active imagination, or else dipping into wishful thinking. "I'm ready," she said briskly.

"Fine." His voice betrayed nothing beyond patience. He stepped back so she could precede him into the hall.

As she passed him, she glanced up and decided to act as if this were the first time they'd met. "Have you ever worked at a small-town paper before?"

He tilted his head as though trying to figure out the reason behind her question. "You know I haven't, Ginny."

It was obvious he wasn't going to let her get away with that ploy, but Ginny went ahead, anyway. She had practiced her little speech all weekend. "It's not the same as what you're used to, you know. A small-town newspaper covers a lot more than simply news. It's the town's identity, its link to the world."

"It's a means of conveying news," Bret said dryly, swinging into step beside her. "No more, no less. It doesn't matter if the news is about a sale at the local variety store or about the mayor taking kickbacks on city building projects. It's news."

"There's a lot more to it than that!"

Bret frowned, and for a moment, she saw the driven man, not the affable stranger. "I know this paper has been in your family for four generations, but it's only a job, not your baby."

She squared her shoulders and clapped her hands onto her hips. "Look who's talking! You *lived* at the office in Memphis when you weren't out with some news source or the vice squad, and I never saw—" She forced herself to stop. It was another old argument, one they'd never resolved.

He riveted his attention on her with the single-mindedness of a hawk swooping down on its prey. "Is that why you left me? Because of my job?"

Ginny waited before answering to make sure her voice wouldn't show how shaky she felt inside. "If we're going to work together, we can't let our personal history enter this office."

"Like hell. What's going to keep it out?"

She didn't say anything. She simply kept control of her emotions and walked past him into the newsroom. Pausing, she pointed with pride to the computer terminals that had been installed a few years ago, then indicated the desks where one full-time and two part-time reporters usually sat. The room was deserted because all three of them were working on the assignments she'd given them the previous week. "The pace is pretty hectic here on Fridays, Mondays and Tuesdays," she said, "because the *Herald* comes out on Wednesdays. Though, of course, it's not as busy as the paper in Memphis."

"Hardly," he murmured as he quickly scanned the desks, computer terminals and fax machine. She suspected his one look was so thorough that he could have drawn the place from memory. "That's why it appeals to me."

"I'm *so* glad," she said, and could have sworn she heard a breath of laughter from him. But his expression was blandly interested when she gave him a sharp glance. She led him into the next room. "Here's the classified department."

Bret questioned her about the advertising rates and suggested raising them. Ginny, who had been considering doing that, wished she'd put it into effect before he came.

The *Herald* was one of the few small-town papers that still had its own presses, ancient though they were. When Ginny took Bret into the large open room where the offset presses were housed, his face lit up. "This place is a mess," he said, looking with undisguised pleasure at the ink-soaked rags and tools lying beside one of the presses.

"It's always like this," Ginny explained, relaxing for a moment when she saw his smile. "Last Friday the pressmen were beating one of the gears with a wrench and swearing at the top of their lungs." She grinned. "It was quite a show."

"Pressmen are a breed unto themselves. Did they fix the gear?"

"I think it started working again purely out of self-defense."

Bret tipped his head back and chuckled. For the briefest instant, Ginny could have closed her eyes and imagined herself back to a time when they had laughed like this often. The sudden change in Bret's expression told her he felt that way, too. Ginny sobered, her laughter dying and leaving an awkward silence.

She met his eyes, and apprehension rose in her. She couldn't be sure, but she thought it was the result of finally being close to the man who haunted her dreams.

His lips twisted in response to the misgivings in her face. "Ginny..." He lifted his hand as if to cup her shoulder, but she stepped back.

Nervously hooking a strand of hair behind her ear, she said, "Come on, I'll show you the darkroom." She nodded toward a heavy door a few feet down the hall-way. "We'll have to be careful . . ."

"I know my way around a darkroom." Bret took her arm and steered her toward the door. After knocking to make sure the room was empty and no film would be ruined by exposure to light, he swung the door open and hustled her inside. "Let's see what kind of equipment we've got here."

"Wait a minute," she protested as she was dragged along. "You have to be—"

"What?" He slammed the door shut. The red safety light made him look like a devil.

"—careful of the door," she finished lamely, then sighed in resignation and rubbed the back of her hand against her forehead. "Congratulations, Bret, you've just locked us in."

He crossed his arms over his chest and leaned against the heavy metal door frame. "I know. Doris told me about the sticky lock."

Ginny stared at him. "Then why on earth did you shut it?"

"So we could talk." Bret reached up and flipped on the overhead fluorescent lights. "I figured the only way I'd get answers was to trap you somewhere."

"Answers?"

"Yes. I want to know why you left me."

# CHAPTER THREE

"OH, BRET. This certainly isn't the time or the place..."

"Okay, then, please tell me when *will* be a good time and place?" He moved from the door frame in a rush, his face showing his frustration and anger. "You wouldn't talk to me last winter when I came after you. I got home from the hospital—the *hospital,* for God's sake—to find the apartment empty and a note from you."

Ginny backed away from him until her spine was pressed against the developing table. She bumped an open tray, and the faint vinegary smell of stop bath tickled her nose. Uneasily she scooted farther along the table's edge. It looked as if she and Bret were going to get into this discussion whether she wanted to or not.

"I'd told you for weeks that I couldn't live with the risks you took and the long hours you worked. Then, when you were hurt in that shoot-out between the police and those drug dealers, I just couldn't take it." Her eyes were full of anguish as she looked up at him. "I made the mistake—"

"Of leaving me! You sure as hell did."

"—of marrying you!"

"You should have stayed and toughed it out!"

Bret had been coming closer, towering over her as they argued, but now he stepped back and regarded her with an expression that was both furious and disgusted. "I thought you married me because you loved me."

Ginny forced herself to move her gaze away from him and down at her hands, which she'd clenched tightly together at her waist. With conscious effort, she loosened them. "I thought I did, too. I was wrong." She looked up, pleading for understanding. "Even though I was twenty-two, I was unbelievably naive. What did I know?"

"You knew how to say, 'I do.'"

"There's more to marriage than just a ceremony."

He spun away from her and stalked across the room. "No kidding. I should have guessed you weren't going to stick around for the long haul when you kept the name McCoy."

"I needed to have my own identity."

"You wouldn't have lost it by changing your name!"

"Yes, I would have, because—"

"Because you didn't trust me," he broke in. "There should be some measure of trust in a marriage."

"Was I supposed to trust you not to get yourself hurt?" she shot back, then held up her hands, palms outward, as she took a deep breath to steady herself. "Never mind. We're only going to get into an argument."

"The latest of many." Sighing in exasperation, Bret ran his hands through his short blond hair.

Although her heart was knocking desperately in her throat, she faced him squarely. "Bret, I don't see how we'll be able to work together."

He raised both brows in mock astonishment. "Oh? Are you planning to quit the *Herald?*"

"Of course not!"

"Well, I'm not leaving. I just got here. And if you leave, you'll be running away—again."

He was right, although she hated to admit it. She stomped to the door and pounded on it, calling for Doris to come let them out. Her brain worked furiously, trying to figure out a way they could both stay. She experienced momentary fury at her father for getting her into this, but rationality returned, forcing her to admit she would have to deal with Bret and her unresolved feelings sooner or later.

She jumped and spun around when he laid a hand on her shoulder. His gray eyes were cool and held just a hint of mockery. "Well, Ginny, what's it to be? Going to run away again?"

"No."

Bret tilted his head to the side as he watched her. He placed his hands on his hips and flexed his shoulders easily. He seemed so sure of himself, while her sweaty fingers gripped the doorknob spasmodically. She wanted to kick him. Instead, she glared at him.

"Well, what are we going to do?" he asked, goading her.

"We're going to work together. We're both professionals. I can handle it if you can."

"As you say—I can if you can. That's one thing that's changed about you."

Ginny was instantly suspicious. "What?"

"You've begun to think of yourself as a professional journalist. When did that happen?"

She had no intention of answering that loaded question, so she knocked on the door once again.

When Bret grabbed her upraised hand, she squeaked in surprise and whipped her head around. "What are you doing?"

"Here's something that hasn't changed. You still bite your nails when you're nervous." He looked up as he ran his thumb along the ragged edges and then over her knuckles. "Now what's made you so nervous, I wonder? Seeing me again?"

She trembled at his touch and quickly pulled her hand away. It was true, but she'd be darned if she was going to admit it. She willed steadiness into her voice. "Bret, we're two adults who happen to be working together. Anything that's gone on between us in our private lives shouldn't be brought to the office."

Bret turned her until she faced him fully. "This is just a small newspaper in rural South Carolina, Ginny, not a giant corporation."

"You know what I mean," she answered shortly.

"You're saying that we can work together—with me as the boss—and not let our private lives affect us?"

"We don't *have* a private life." As she caught sight of his laughing eyes, her gaze skittered away from his. "At least, not together."

"Okay, then. You're saying our separate lives outside of work can be kept just that—separate?"

Ginny had the distinct feeling there was a trap somewhere in his reasoning, but she nodded slowly. "That's right. We won't see each other away from the office, so our past won't matter."

He shrugged. "Maybe, maybe not. We'll see."

Ginny started to ask him what he meant, but at that moment Doris swung open the door.

"Sorry," she said, looking from Bret's bland smile to Ginny's flushed face, then back. "The phone rang just when I heard you knocking, and I couldn't get away."

"That's okay," Bret said, holding the door for Ginny and motioning her out with a wave of his hand. "Why don't you call that locksmith again and see if he can get here today?"

"Sure, Bret." Doris gave Ginny a curious look and hurried off to do as her new boss had suggested.

Ginny didn't really notice. She was too busy pulling together her scattered senses and being grateful that she was out of the small room. In the hallway she waited for Bret to continue their discussion, but he merely said, "I have to get settled in my office. Why don't you call a staff meeting for nine so I can meet them? Also, can you bring me copies of the *Herald* for the past two months? I want to see what regular features you run and what projects you've been working on."

Ginny, caught off guard by his businesslike tone, could only nod. "All right, Bret."

Waving carelessly, he turned away and said, "Good. See you later. Call me when everyone's assembled."

He rounded the corner, and Ginny slumped against the wall to catch her breath. This was turning out to be harder than she'd expected. She knew she was right, though. Matters between them would be much easier if they kept their relationship strictly professional and didn't see each other socially. That decided, she headed to the storeroom where back issues of the paper were kept. Her only problem was the strange hollow feeling around her heart.

THE YELLOW GEORGIAN-STYLE house had never looked so welcome. Late-afternoon shadows cast by a willow tree were snaking across the front lawn toward the solidly built home that had been in her family for three generations.

The day's heat was finally giving way to blessed coolness, which perked up Ginny's waning strength. Glad to be home, she parked in her usual spot in the double garage and noticed that Hugh's car was gone.

"You coward," she muttered to her absent parent, hitching her bag onto her shoulder and climbing wearily from the car. "You're still ducking me, aren't you?"

Inside the house she put together a chicken casserole and salad for dinner. The backyard swimming pool reflected ribbons of light through the kitchen window while she worked, reminding her that with fall coming, she wouldn't have many more days to swim.

As soon as she had placed the casserole in the oven and set the timer she went upstairs where she changed into a neon green-and-purple one-piece suit. She pulled her chin-length hair into a ponytail, then stuffed it into a bathing cap, scooped up an oversize towel and hurried down to the pool.

With her first plunge into the water, Ginny felt her tenseness ease. She swam several laps, reveling in the sensation of cool water sliding over heated skin. She loved the freedom of movement she had when swimming. After a while she flipped onto her back and floated, eyes closed, limbs moving languidly.

She decided the day hadn't gone too badly. As expected, she'd received a number of curious looks and even questions from the other staff members. They were concerned about the advisability of her ex-husband's running the paper her family owned. She had simply answered that it was a decision her father had made and she'd have no trouble living with it. To her relief, that seemed to stop the questions. She knew, of course, that the news would be all over Webster in no time.

At the staff meeting Bret had been friendly yet businesslike. She had sat in the back of the room, watching and listening, trying to reconcile this new Bret with the man she'd married. He seemed to have lost the fire, the ambition, that had burned in him. He had been calm and self-assured, impressing the staff with his plans for the *Herald* and impressing her with the changes in him.

Although Ginny still felt like a failure and was upset with Hugh over the way he'd handled it, she was secretly relieved that the burden of the paper was off her shoulders. Bret had taken it from her, as easily and quickly as he had taken her in his arms and danced off with her on the day they'd met.

Ginny dragged her thoughts away from that memory and back to recollections of the staff meeting.

The other reporters respected Bret's knowledge and experience, the pressmen were thrilled to have a man running things again, and the women in the classified section appeared ready to be his slaves for life.

At the thought of their avid interest in Bret, and her own spurt of ridiculous jealousy, Ginny rolled over and dove straight down, swimming an impatient lap underwater, then coming up briefly for air and diving again. She repeated this process half-a-dozen times, intent on working out her emotions as she worked her body.

Finally she swam to the side, surfaced and reached for the brick apron that ran around the perimeter of the pool. Her hand came down on a shoe. Startled, she blinked away the chlorine-treated water stinging her eyes and looked up to see Bret Calhoun.

He was crouched down, resting easily on the balls of his feet, with his forearms propped on his thighs and his hands clasped between them. His lips curved in a grin and his eyes laughed down at her as he said, "Hi, honey, I'm home. Need help with dinner?"

Her mouth gaped open until she felt it filling with water, then she sputtered. "B-Bret, what are you doing here?"

"Offering to help with dinner." He looked around with real interest, then indicated the pansies and petunias she had planted on the other side of the pool. "I see you've been gardening. I brought along that bromeliad we bought on our honeymoon. It's at Sam and Laura's. I'll bring it by."

He couldn't have said anything more calculated to throw her off balance. Instantly she recalled the night they'd bought it, laughing over its big flat leaves and bulbous spiky flower. "That isn't necessary," she protested, gripping the edge of the pool.

He only smiled, smugly, like the Cheshire cat.

Ginny wanted to put her head down on the bricks and weep. Instead, she asked, "Why did you say you stopped by? Something wrong at the paper?"

"He's my guest," Hugh said from nearby.

She drifted back in the water until she could see around Bret. Her father hovered next to the door. That was wise. If she could have reached him, she would have strangled him.

"Hello, Dad. I wondered where you were hiding." She nodded toward Bret and congratulated herself on how reasonable she sounded. "You invited him to dinner?"

"For more than that, actually," Bret interrupted. "You know, it's rude to talk about people as if they're not there."

Suspiciously Ginny held herself away from the side of the pool and bobbed gently in the water as she stared up at him. "What do you mean, 'more than that'?"

"I'm going to rent the apartment over the garage." He smiled again, obviously trying to look harmless.

*"What?"*

"It's true. Hugh says it's just sitting there empty and I might as well use it."

There was a furnished studio apartment above the two-car detached garage that, until recently, had been rented by Diana Sheldon, the art teacher at the local junior high. It had been vacant since she'd been offered the use of a small house owned by the school district.

"Oh, really." She turned her attention from Bret, who somehow managed to look triumphant and sympathetic at the same time, to Hugh. "Dad, could I speak to you, please?" she asked in a tight voice.

"Sure, honey. What is it?" Hugh smiled a slightly puzzled smile as if he couldn't quite fathom why she sounded upset.

Ginny's lips pinched together. For a smart man, her father had been remarkably dense lately. "In the house," she said, jerking her head in that direction.

Noting the stiffness in her face, Hugh nodded cautiously and moved to open the door. "Excuse us a minute, will you, Bret?"

"Of course." Bret's voice was friendly, but his glance wasn't. Then he drew his bottom lip under his teeth as if trying to control the spread of his grin.

Ginny placed her hands on the pool's edge and started to lift herself out of the water. Too late, she realized that she should have swum to the steps in the shallow end, because Bret was reaching down to help. Although it nearly made her topple into the water, she shook him off. "I can do this myself, thanks."

His brows lifted at her frosty tone, but he stepped back, watching her closely as she climbed out, sleek with water and in an obvious temper. Aware of his scrutiny, Ginny grabbed her towel and swirled it around herself with all the aplomb of a bullfighter unfurling his cape. She led the way into the kitchen and closed the door carefully behind herself and Hugh.

Once she was sure their visitor couldn't overhear, she ignored the puddle she was forming and turned on her father. "Dad—"

"Now, honey, don't look at me like I've just let a fox into the henhouse."

"*Let* him in? You've given him a lease! Why did you ask him to stay here? I thought he'd stay with Sam and Laura."

Hugh held up his hands, apparently trying to calm her. "Now, honey, you know that wouldn't work, not with a baby on the way. Besides, Laura twisted her ankle this afternoon and has to keep off of it for a while. Sam and Bret are afraid she'll do too much if he's staying there. Since Sam works at home, he can help her, but Bret needed a place of his own."

Ginny sympathized with her former sister-in-law, whom she knew was already miserable in her last months of pregnancy. "Oh. Well, I'm sorry about that. I can understand Laura's not being able to handle it, but why does Bret have to come *here?* There is a motel in this town, you know. Can't he get a room there or. . . or rent an apartment?''

Her father nodded cheerfully, as if she'd finally come around to his way of thinking. ''Why, that's just what he's doing—renting the apartment over the garage. In fact, he's ready to move in.''

''Oh, joy.''

''I can't understand why this bothers you.''

''Lately, there seems to be a lot you don't understand, Dad.'' Exasperated, she reached up and snatched the swimming cap from her head, then undid her ponytail. Fluffing her hair, she pulled out a corner of her towel and crouched down to wipe up the water that had dripped from her legs.

While she scrubbed, she felt a pinching tightness behind her eyes. The past three days had been a disaster from beginning to end. It was as if she had no place to turn and no one to talk to. Feeling a gentle hand on her head, she forced back the tears. ''I don't know why you're doing all this.''

Hugh's voice was low and full of love. ''It's silly to have an empty apartment when someone can use it. Anyway, you said you could work with Bret. Doesn't that mean you can live next door to him, too?''

''This is more than next door,'' she protested, standing and giving Hugh an incredulous look.

''What's the difference? Maybe you made a mistake when you left him, but that's ancient history now, right?''

''I didn't make a mistake! Dad, if you'll remember, you were beside yourself when Bret and I got married. You tried to talk us out of it. You didn't seem particularly upset when I came home last winter.''

"I was half-dead with pneumonia. I couldn't spare the energy to get upset about anything. Like I said, your marriage is ancient history, right?"

"Right." Her answer sounded uncertain even to her own ears, so she cleared her throat and spoke more firmly, adding a nod for emphasis. "Right!"

"He'll have his own life, his own friends, probably girlfriends, too. You'll hardly see him, except at the office."

Ginny knew that was true, but why did the thought make her so uncomfortable?

Irritated by her ambivalent feelings, she gathered her towel more tightly around her body. Even if Hugh's tactics weren't the best, there was truth to what he said. But privately, she wondered if his illness had affected his mind a little. She'd never known him to be this insensitive or ready to point out her mistakes. Another thought came to her and she looked at her father through narrowed eyes. "Dad, you wouldn't, by any chance, be trying to get Bret and me together again, would you?"

Obviously hurt, he drew back. Ginny began having twinges of guilt even before he said, "Of course not! If I'd been trying that, I would have made you go back to him and work things out last winter."

Ginny threw her hands into the air. "You just said you couldn't have, Dad. You could hardly lift your head off the pillow, remember?"

"Well, maybe so, but you have to admit that I've never interfered with your decisions, not since you were in high school."

"That's true," she agreed reluctantly, wondering what he was leading up to.

"I know you're a mature woman who thinks things out carefully and weighs all the options. You never would have left your husband unless you had a good reason. I respected your right not to talk about it if you didn't want to, didn't I?"

Ginny examined his expression, trying to feel reassured, but there was something in his tone that nagged at her. Hugh had made his living with words, and she had difficulty believing he was just pointing out his own good character traits. "Yes, you did."

"So, why would you think I'm going to change now? Don't you think there's a remote possibility that I'm renting the apartment to Bret because it's empty and it'll give us a little extra income?"

She lifted her hand to her mouth and nibbled thoughtfully on her thumbnail. "I suppose that's possible."

Hugh coughed, catching her full attention. "See? My motives are completely aboveboard." He beamed at her, then coughed again.

"Dad, have you seen Dr. Clay?"

He brushed off her reaching hands, then patted her shoulder awkwardly. "Nah, I'm all right." But his coughing continued, hard enough to cause tears to roll down his cheeks and turn his face cherry red. When the fit passed, he wheezed, "I think I should rest a little before dinner." He gave her a wan look. "If that's okay with you?"

She hitched her towel up with one hand and took his arm with the other. "Of course, Dad, of course. But I don't understand why you're having this relapse," she fussed, helping him to the foot of the stairs. "One minute you're fine and the next you're coughing until you're red in the face!"

He shook his head. "That's just the way this seems to go, honey. All I need is rest, though," he added hastily. His face held a long-suffering expression as he laid a hand on the maple banister and began a slow ascent. "You'll help Bret settle in, won't you?"

"Sure, Dad, don't worry about a thing." Distraught, she followed on his heels as he dragged himself wearily up the stairs. "But I still think you should go to see the doctor."

"No, no. I'll be fine."

"Can I get you anything?"

"Just take care of Bret." Hugh disappeared into his room and shut the door.

Ginny went to her own room, and it wasn't until she was getting out of her suit that she realized how cleverly she'd been manipulated.

Once Hugh had started coughing, she'd dropped all her objections and done exactly what he wanted. He probably wasn't all that sick, yet his cough sounded genuine and the redness of his face truly frightened her. She remembered well what it had been like when her mother had died. The thought of Hugh's being gone filled her with panic.

She wrapped the towel around herself and reached for the phone on the nightstand. She punched out the number of the doctor who had cared for them for years. When he answered, Dr. Clay assured her that Hugh should be completely recovered, but urged Ginny to have him come in for a checkup. He also said Hugh should avoid stress. She hung up, knowing she had very little chance of convincing Hugh to go for an examination. He kept swearing he was fine. Besides, her father didn't need to worry about avoiding stress— he didn't suffer from it, he *caused* it!

As she mulled over various ways to get her father in to see the doctor, Ginny pulled on a pair of jeans and a buttercup-yellow campshirt. After sliding her feet into sandals and running a brush through her hair, she went back downstairs. To her surprise, Bret was in the kitchen, competently removing the bubbling casserole from the oven.

"New recipe?" he asked, sniffing with deep appreciation as he set the dish down on the ceramic-tiled countertop.

Ginny had to compose herself before answering. "No, it was one of my mother's."

"You never made it when we were married." He leaned a hip against the counter and slapped a pot holder against his palm while he lazily inspected her slim figure.

Ginny's skin tingled as if he had touched her, but she drew her lips together angrily. "I made it often—you just weren't ever home to eat it."

He lifted a brow in acknowledgment of her direct hit. "My mistake. Suppose you let me try it out now, hmm?"

"Certainly. You'll find a plate in the cupboard above the sink. Silverware's in the drawer just below it." She headed for the back door.

He caught her wrist as she passed. "Where are you going?"

"To get the apartment ready."

"Why don't you join me for dinner since you made it? You've worked hard today. I know you're hungry."

She was, but it had little to do with a need for food. Alarmed by her body's unbidden reaction to his closeness, she arched away from him. "Let me go, Bret."

His eyes gleamed with humor. "But this is so pleasant." He settled his other hand on her waist, but allowed her a few more inches of space.

"Not for me."

"Would you rather run away again?"

That stopped her. "From my own home? Hardly."

"I thought your home was with me. At least, that's what the wedding vows said."

"Yes, Bret," she said sweetly. "Except, you were never *at* home."

He smiled in the slow, breath-robbing way that had once made her feel as if she was the center of his universe. "I'm home now, Ginny."

The seductive tone in his voice told her to trust him—but she couldn't. "I find that hard to believe."

"Only time will tell."

"That was the problem, wasn't it?" she said, deliberately twisting his words. "You obviously couldn't tell time." Oh, she hated the way she sounded, somewhere between spite and self-pity. Taking him unawares, she spun out of his light grasp. "I don't want to get into this now, okay?"

"You're only delaying the inevitable."

"Then I'll delay it indefinitely. I may have to work with you—all right, for you—but our...our past is just that." She stumbled over the words, surprised at how much pain she still felt. "It's past and...and completely separate from our working relationship."

"You think so? Seems to me you said the same thing in the darkroom today."

"A lot of good it did me. You obviously didn't listen."

"I never listen when you talk nonsense. You know that." He glanced around. "Where's Hugh?"

Glad to shift the focus of their conversation, she said, "Upstairs lying down. He still coughs sometimes and has spells of weakness."

"Hasn't really recovered?"

"I thought he had, but lately he seems worse, and the stubborn old goat won't go to the doctor."

Bret took her hand as if to offer comfort. "He'll be okay now that he's retiring. He'll have plenty of time to rest. Hey, why don't we wait dinner on him? In the meantime, we can start moving my things into the apartment. Where's the key?"

"On the rack by the door," she answered as he pulled her along with him. He waited while she plucked the key from its hook, then spun her around and headed toward the front of the house. That was one thing about Bret that certainly hadn't changed. When he wanted something, nothing stood in his way. The rest of the world might as well bend to his will.

Outside, she stopped short at the sight of the sporty red Geo parked on the street. When they'd been married, Bret had owned a small pickup truck. It would have been far more appropriate for a move than this little thing, which was packed to the roof with clothes. She wondered if this move was as permanent as he claimed. He couldn't have possibly brought all his possessions with him.

Bret misread her expression. "I had to sell the truck. It dropped its transmission. Sold it to a kid who wanted to fix it up." He sighed theatrically as he unlocked the door and reached to grab some clothes and hangers. "I know what you're thinking—the bench seat in the truck was perfect for making out, and these bucket jobs will probably give us both backaches. But if you get the urge for some serious hanky-panky just let me know. I'm sure we can manage something.''

She blushed from shoulder to scalp. ''Oh, don't be an idiot,'' she said, hiding her face behind the stack of shirts and jackets he'd handed her. The combination of his teasing and the painfully familiar scent rising from his clothing sent such a wave of nostalgia through her she felt a momentary weakness. In her deepest bouts of loneliness they were two of the things she missed most. He'd probably given her these clothes to carry deliberately, the rat.

She straightened, determined not to be affected by him. Firmly, she turned her mind to the stuffy bachelor apartment he would soon occupy. She wondered if she should tell him about the redecorating Diana Sheldon had done. No, she'd let it be a surprise.

She walked purposefully toward the garage, but called back over her shoulder, ''You know, it'll be easier to unload this stuff if you move your car around and park it by the garage.''

''Okay,'' he agreed, much too easily. ''You're the boss.''

''That'll be the day,'' she muttered. She hadn't been the master of her own fate for the past three days.

With the load of clothes settled on one hip and her head tilted so that she could see her feet, she climbed the sixteen steps to the garage apartment. As soon as she reached the landing she juggled the stack in her arms to free one hand, unlocked the door and swung it open. She wrinkled her nose at the musty smell and crossed the room to lay the jackets and shirts across the camelback sofa. She glanced at the furniture, which was plain, but clean and serviceable. There was nothing to brag about, but nothing to complain about, either. She moved to open the miniblinds and windows. By the time she'd finished, Bret was on his way up the stairs.

"Hey, Ginny, get the door, will you? My—Good Lord!"

She rushed to hold the screen door as he entered with his arms full. It would have been impossible to hide the impish smile caused by the sight of his astounded face, so she didn't bother to try.

"I think that Dad forgot to mention something," she said in a voice that fought not to giggle. She relieved him of his burden, then watched as his arms fell limply to his sides. Bret looked slowly around the room, stopped, started and stopped again.

For the first time that day, Ginny felt as if she was in control. Smugly, she turned to view the room, although she had already gazed on it in stupefied wonder many times.

The apartment's floor, walls and ceiling were covered with unique murals. The four walls had identical windows. Over, under and around each of them were painted maple trees representing the four seasons. Winter had bare spiky branches bending under sheets of ice so thick and cold-looking they made the viewer feel frostbitten. With the merest hint of yellow-green buds and the presence of wet-winged newly emerging butterflies on the next set of trees, spring was perfectly depicted. The summer wall was thick with leaves of jewel-like emerald green. Tiny animals hid among the branches as if wary of intruders. Fall was the most wonderful, though, with rich yellows, golds and reds painted in dizzying profusion across the wall.

Ginny saw Bret swallow before gazing up at the ceiling, partitioned into four equal triangles. Each was different—one painted a cold gray and the other three in varying shades of blue. Clouds, birds and butter-flies fought for space in the crowded sky.

Then Bret looked at the floor—and started in sur-prise when he saw a gopher staring up at him from a large knothole in the pine floor. Other woodland creatures played, slept or grazed everywhere on the flat surface.

After he'd taken it all in, he turned to Ginny and gaped at her. "Did you do this?"

"I wish. Well, I helped. Diana Sheldon did it. When I could leave Dad on his own I came over here and helped." The minute tedious work, done to the art-ist's exacting standards, had been therapeutic for Ginny, taking her mind off Hugh's illness—and the husband she had left.

Bret lifted his hands helplessly to encompass the area. "Hugh didn't mind?"

"He paid for the paint."

"Is this Diana Sheldon a bit . . . eccentric?"

"She's a fruitcake."

Bret laughed.

"Seriously." Ginny gathered up the armload of clothes she'd taken from Bret and headed for the closet, which had louvered doors cleverly painted to resemble a dead tree. "She teaches art at the junior high. Obviously spending the last five years with bud-ding thirteen-year-old artists has unhinged her mind."

"No kidding." Bret followed with more of his things and they stood, hip to hip, arranging hangers in the closet. Ginny had a fleeting memory of the time he'd made room for her and helped her hang her things in the closet of his classy Memphis apartment.

"This was very clever of you, Ginny," he complimented.

"What was?" she asked, turning to him with her face full of innocence.

"Not telling me about this god-awful woodland bower."

She grinned. "But I assumed Dad had told you all about it. The two of you seemed so—" she puckered her face comically "—chummy. And it's not god-awful. Diana is immensely proud of it. I wrote an article about it for the *Herald*. She wants to bring each new art class to see it. In fact, since school started a couple of weeks ago, you'll probably have company soon."

"Great. I'll be sure to bake cookies."

She looked at him and laughed. The day's shocks were temporarily forgotten as Bret's handsome face creased into an answering grin.

For a moment warmth flowed between them, sweeping her back to a time when everything had seemed as full of promise as the painting of spring across the room. But it was an illusion. Behind that mural was a plain plaster wall, and behind her memories was an ocean of hurt.

Ginny shifted her gaze, then stepped away. "Did you move your car?"

"Yes." Bret held out a hand to stop her. "Ginny..."

"Hey, aren't you two finished? I'm starved." Hugh bounded to the top of the stairs.

Grateful for the interruption, Ginny hurried to the door. "I thought you were going to rest."

"I did."

"For a full thirty minutes."

"What's the matter, Ginny girl? Something happening up here you don't want me to know about?" His attention went from her to Bret and back again.

"No, I just thought... Oh, never mind." It was impossible for her to win an argument with him anymore, so why should she bother to try? Hearing Bret coming up behind her, she stepped toward her father. Then she placed her hands on his shoulders and urged him into the room. "Since you're feeling better, why don't *you* help Bret? I'll get dinner on the table."

As she hastily started down the wooden stairs, Ginny slipped. Before she could even clutch the railing, an arm went around her waist to steady her.

"Careful, Ginny. There's no hurry," Bret said, his warm breath caressing her ear. "We have all the time in the world."

That was what she was afraid of. She pulled from his grasp, then glanced back at him. He was watching her, his smile one of sympathy, as if he knew she wanted to run but realized there was no place to go. She'd be seeing him every day at work, taking orders from him. Then she'd come home, and he'd be there, too. Only her pride kept her from admitting she couldn't handle the situation.

She turned away from him and, back straight and head high, walked serenely down the stairs and into the house.

# CHAPTER FOUR

"YOU CAN'T STOP PRINTING the school lunch menu just like that!" Ginny snapped her fingers an inch from Bret's nose.

He didn't flinch. In fact, he leaned closer until they were eyeball to eyeball over the mounds of paper on his desk. "Of course I can."

"But it's been featured every week of the school year..."

"Since the carpetbaggers like me moved in during Reconstruction, no doubt."

At another time Ginny would have laughed at Bret's aligning himself with the brash Northerners who had moved south in search of fast and easy profits after the War between the States. After all, Bret had been born and raised in the South. But right now she was too upset to find any humor in the situation. In the two weeks since Bret had taken over the paper, he'd made more changes than she had teeth.

"It's a small thing," she protested, drawing back oh-so-slightly as the scent of Bret's spicy after-shave assailed her. She had quickly discovered that even a whiff of it conjured up memories guaranteed to take the starch out of her knees. "It fills very little space in the *Herald* and provides a service to the community."

"But it isn't needed and hasn't been for a long time. The school sends monthly menus home to the parents."

"Which the kids promptly lose."

Bret shrugged. "Hey, that's not my problem."

She put clenched hands on her hips. "No, *your* problem is that you want to do away with an established tradition."

"Which no longer serves a purpose." He rocked back on his heels and rested his fists on his hips, matching her pose. "You know, instead of fighting me, you could think of some use for the space."

"Such as?"

"Such as featuring an outstanding student or teacher every week. Did you know that one of the high-school seniors has a good chance of being accepted at West Point? Some kid named Biggs."

"Well, no." She blinked in surprised pleasure as she relaxed her posture. "Jeffrey Biggs? That's wonderful. He was in Carrie's geometry class last year." Her voice was rich with skepticism. "Where did you get this information?"

"At the Rotary Club breakfast. I sat next to the proud father."

"Oh."

That was another thing that unsettled her. She'd fully expected Bret to become bored with the slow pace of Webster and the *Herald* after a few days, but he hadn't. She would have bet that he'd be unable to leave behind the rush of excitement he received from working with the Memphis vice squad—and taking chances with his life.

So far he had proved her wrong. He'd joined a number of civic organizations and seemed content to attend their functions alone or with either his brother or Hugh. She knew his evenings were often spent at Sam and Laura's house, though she could have kicked herself for being so aware of his movements *and* for her secret wish that she was included in them.

He had brought the bromeliad to her, and she'd been pleased to see it was flourishing. It now sat on her dresser, taking up too much space and reminding her of their honeymoon. In a way it was like having a piece of Bret in her bedroom. She could move the plant, but what was the use? Bret would still be in her thoughts.

Other than his first day at the *Herald*, when he had trapped her in the darkroom, he hadn't tried to find out why she'd left him. Knowing how persistent he could be, she was relieved and delighted that he'd let the subject drop.

In the office, they had already developed a remarkably congenial working relationship. Although she hadn't admitted it to anyone, especially not to her father, she was glad to be free of responsibility for the paper.

But Bret seemed to understand that she was having a hard time giving up control and had consulted her on all major decisions—and even some small ones. Like today's discussion about the school lunch menu. She felt a little petty for objecting, but the service had been part of the *Herald* since before she'd been born.

Bret had taken a number of her suggestions, though, even the one about having Webster citizens write guest editorials concerning world events. The first one would be printed next week. He was also giving her space for a column of her own. She could use it to discuss whatever she wished, and for that, she was grateful. She wasn't grateful, however, for the way his presence constantly disturbed her. She'd been so sure she could handle it. After all, she'd had several months to get over him.

And yet she always knew when he was in the building. She could sense him even before she saw him. His clothing seemed to have been chosen strictly to upset her equilibrium. He wore snug jeans and shirts that he'd once teamed with his tailored suits, although now the shirts looked comfortable, instead of starched and crisp. Her fingers itched to touch them. It was his very casualness that she found so irresistible, which mystified her. She didn't love him anymore. Why was he so much on her mind?

She thought she'd come up with an explanation. While in the office, his presence, voice, *scent* seemed to be everywhere. And all of them were affecting her at the moment.

Ginny eased away from Bret a bit more. "It's nice that Jeff might go to West Point and it's nice that you want to feature articles about the students, but—"

"I'm glad you agree," he said, apparently amused by her reaction. "Since the decision is already made."

"Then why did you call me in here?"

His shrug was nonchalant, yet challenging. "So I could watch you explode. I haven't quite made up my mind, but I think I like it better when you disagree with me. It shows that you're developing a mind of your own in this profession."

"Well, bully for me."

"Of course, you've always had a mind of your own when it comes to personal relationships, haven't you?"

Ginny didn't dignify that with an answer. Bret went on, "I've been thinking about doing a series of articles concerning the area schools, anyway. In fact, the high school is having open house tonight. And you and I are going.''

''Whatever for?''

''To interview some parents, some students, teachers.'' When she started to protest, he held up his hand. ''Don't tell me you're afraid to be alone with me?''

That brought her pride flying out to stiffen her resolve. She stuffed her hands into the pockets of the slim denim skirt she wore. ''Certainly not!''

''Then you won't mind coming? I'll pick you up at six-thirty. If all goes well, we might be able to talk the high-school principal into letting you pose as a student and spend a few days visiting classes.''

''Not on your life! I've done my time in that school.''

Bret grinned at her. ''I was kidding, Ginny.''

She ran her fingers through her hair and pulled it away from her face. ''I knew that.''

This time he laughed out loud, and she answered with a self-conscious grin. For a moment warmth flowed between them. She should have remembered how he'd loved to tease her and her reaction to it. When they were married, she'd been too darned determined to hold her own with him to ever laugh at herself. She'd been too frightened that, because he was so much more sophisticated and successful than she, he would lose interest in her. Of course, that had happened, anyway.

Things were different between them now, though. He still teased her and argued with her, but she fought back, managing to make her opinions known. He seemed to respect her for that, too.

Thinking about those changes, she glanced down at the piles of mail on his desk. One thick manila envelope was stamped with the return address of the Memphis daily where Bret had worked for so many years. Newspaper clippings were spilling out of it. A note was attached. She only had to turn her head slightly to read, "See what you're missing?"

"Messages from home?" She asked flippantly, hoping to hide her discomfort at the sudden reminder that he probably wouldn't be in Webster for long.

The friendly teasing faded from Bret's eyes. "I *am* home, Ginny, whether you choose to believe that or not. The note's from Frank Brevard."

"Your editor? He obviously wants you back."

"Former editor," Bret corrected automatically. "The question is, what do *you* want, Ginny?"

That was an easy one. She wanted to be immune to Bret. She wanted him to take his crooked Calhoun smile, his Southern gentleman's charm and his darned spicy cologne and devastate some other woman with them. She wasn't interested! Ginny firmly told herself all this while her stomach took a sickening dip at the thought of him doing that very thing. "I want to be left alone to do my job, just as I'm sure you'd like to be left alone to do yours."

"Oh, of course, Ginny." His tone was drenched with grave agreement.

She nodded, then hooked a strand of hair behind her ear. To her amazement, she realized that her fingers were shaking. "Well, good. As long as we understand each other." She cast another curious look at the envelope before she turned away.

"Would you like to read the articles, Ginny? I think you'd find them interesting." Bret shoved the clippings back into the envelope and held it up, giving it an inviting waggle. "No? Suit yourself. Don't say I didn't offer."

Again, there was something in his voice that made her wary. She felt the way she had two weeks ago when he'd promised that their relationship inside the office would be strictly professional—but had failed to add anything about their relationship outside the office. Though she knew it was cowardly, she didn't want to press him. Instead, she headed back to her own office where she shut the door, collapsed into her creaky chair and tried to do some work. But she accomplished little. Her tingling nerves continually reminded her they were going somewhere together. It wasn't a date, of course, but she was looking forward to it.

THAT EVENING, when she'd changed clothes three times and was still ready ten minutes early, she decided she needed a distraction and went in search of her father. She found a note from him on the kitchen table saying he'd gone to play cards with a few friends.

She read the note ruefully, then tossed it into the trash. He was continuing to hide from her, though she didn't know why. She felt she'd adjusted well to the changes he'd forced on her.

Aimlessly she picked up the dishcloth and took a few swipes at the spotless chrome on the front of the oven, then ended up by the window, looking out at the stairs to the garage apartment. She propped her elbow on the sill and began nibbling her fingernails. With a sound of disgust she snatched her hand away and reached for the telephone to call Carrie.

When she heard her sister's voice Ginny smiled and hitched the kitchen stool closer so she could settle in for a chat.

"How's it going?" she asked, and listened with pleasure as Carrie described her classes, professors and the new friends she was making. She sounded happy, though a bit homesick, and Ginny told her how much they missed her.

"So, what's this I hear about Bret's living over the garage?" Carrie asked her finally.

"You think that was my idea?" Ginny sighed. "You've been talking to Dad? He didn't tell me."

"Are you surprised?"

"No. He's been ducking me for two weeks. As often as I see him, you'd think we lived in separate states."

"He's probably feeling guilty."

"Fat chance."

"Well, maybe not," Carrie admitted with a laugh, then her voice sobered. "Is it hard having Bret there?"

"Yes," Ginny groaned, and this time they both laughed. Having Bret there was also exhilarating and frustrating and scary, she added silently. She felt as if she was teetering on the edge of either a wonderful discovery or a disastrous mistake.

"Why do you think Bret accepted the job?"

"He says he wants to take things slower." Ginny wound the phone cord around her fingers and glanced toward the back door.

"Do you believe him?"

"I'm not sure. Sometimes I think I understand him, but then he turns around and does something that surprises me. It just proves my point that I didn't know him at all when I married him."

"So what's stopping you from getting to know him better now?"

That question brought Ginny's confused thoughts to a rocking halt. What, indeed? She knew the answer. It was her fear of being hurt again. Before she could voice it Bret knocked at the door. Ginny said goodbye hastily and hung up, hurrying to get her purse and lock the house. She couldn't lock out Carrie's question, though. It had stolen through her defenses and created havoc in her mind.

THE REDBRICK HIGH SCHOOL was lit up the way it had been on many occasions during the years Ginny and her sister had attended it. Because the school had been built in the early sixties, when administrators hadn't worried about vandalism, each classroom had huge windows with dark shades to block out the sun if a class needed to view a film or video.

Ginny paused at the bottom of the steps to examine the building. She was very aware of Bret as he stood beside her. She wryly admitted to herself that he probably knew she'd chosen to wear her pale pink sweaterdress because he used to tell her he liked her in pink.

He placed one wide palm on the small of her back and bent over her solicitously when she stopped. "Is something wrong?"

"No, not really. It's just . . . Did you know I started here when I was only twelve?" she blurted, then wondered why. She tried never to think about that foolish episode, even though the foolishness had been that of the school administration, not hers.

"You're kidding! Why?"

Now she regretted mentioning it, but she could tell by his intense interest he wasn't going to let her change the subject. "I started kindergarten before my fifth birthday, and when I got to junior high, my teacher and the principal decided I was ready to go on to high school."

"And were you?"

Ginny shook her head, marveling at the guilt she still felt. "No, I wasn't, but I should have been. The classes were pretty easy for me, especially math. But my mother had just died and—" she shrugged "—I guess I couldn't handle things all that well..."

"You were only a kid, for heaven's sake," Bret exclaimed. "What did people expect of you?"

Surprised by the vehemence in his voice, she glanced up. A hint of a blush colored her fair skin. "I'd always been a straight-A student. They must have felt that I wasn't being challenged in school. They soon found out they'd made a mistake and sent me back to my own grade level. No harm was done."

Bret's eyes narrowed. "I wonder," he murmured.

Wishing she hadn't brought the subject up, Ginny flashed him an ironic smile, then climbed several steps before realizing Bret wasn't with her. She glanced over her shoulder. He was standing with one foot on a stair and one hand on the rail as he gazed at her.

Her smile died. "What's wrong? Have I got a spot on my dress?" She pinched the fabric and stretched it away from her waist.

Slowly he came up to join her. When he reached her side he crooked his forefinger under her chin and lifted it until she was looking at him. There was something in his eyes she couldn't quite identify. Tenderness she'd certainly seen before, but never this compassion.

Against her will and all her good sense, she began to tremble.

"Nothing's wrong, but I think I finally understand something about you."

"What's that?"

"How much everyone expected of you." A group of people were pushing past them with curious looks. "We'll finish this later," he promised.

Feeling a bit silly, Ginny pulled away from him. But Bret took her arm and they followed the crowd. "Just think," he said in a lighter tone. "If we'd stayed married, this could be us in twenty years."

"Us?" Her voice squeaked, still affected by the moment they'd shared. She cleared her throat and tried to match his bantering tone. "Why us?"

"Because by then we would have had Bret and Ginny juniors."

"Oh?" She frowned. Their only discussion concerning children had ended with the decision to put off parenthood for several years. She'd only been twenty-two, after all, and a recent college graduate. Still, she often felt a small pang of regret that she hadn't had his child. It would have made the divorce that much harder, but the unreasonable longing persisted.

"Sure. We'd be going to talk to little Bret's teachers, sure our son was doing well in his studies only to discover he's more interested in girls and football than algebra and English."

"We would?"

"Of course. He'd be just like me."

"I shudder at the thought."

"Smart mouth." Bret pushed the door open for her and held it while she entered, then followed her. "Little Ginny, however, would be a model student, and beautiful, too. I'd have to spend my nights standing by the front door with a shotgun ready to guard her honor."

Ginny laughed at him. "You'd be a very naive father, then. She might not want her honor guarded."

"No matter, I'd still do it."

Their banter continued as they walked through the building to the auditorium where the parents were greeted, then directed to their children's respective classes. Bret and Ginny both pulled out small notebooks, which they used to make observations of the proceedings. They separated and went off to interview parents and teachers. Ginny found herself enthusiastically falling in with Bret's plan, deciding this was a good idea, after all. She knew that children who were lucky enough to have parents participating in their schooling were the best students. This article, and the column she intended to write on the subject, might encourage more parents to become involved. She spotted Bret in the hallway and started toward him to compliment him on his idea.

He smiled when he saw her coming and flattened himself against some lockers, out of the stream of traffic, to wait until she joined him. Then she saw a man approach him and give him an enthusiastic clap on the shoulder. Ginny recognized him as the father of Jeffrey Biggs, the boy being considered for West Point.

"Hey, Calhoun, I was talking to your brother today. Congratulations on the—"

Bret grabbed the man's arm and spun him away. The two of them were swallowed by the crowd, leaving Ginny gaping after them. What had that been about?

She asked him when he joined her later, but he said, "I'd rather discuss it when we're alone. You might make a scene."

"I might what?"

"See? You're starting one already." He indicated a door behind her. "Why don't you talk to that group of parents over there?" he suggested. "I'll go to that classroom down the hall. There's a bunch of people in there with name tags. Must be faculty. Maybe I'll get some quotes."

He strode away, leaving her alone. She couldn't imagine what was going on, but she intended to find out. Dutifully she returned to work.

Within an hour, the crowd had begun to thin, and Ginny found Bret near the front doors. The people around him dispersed instantly when she approached, apparently at some signal from Bret, who pushed the door open with one hand and guided her outside with the other.

Once they were inside his sporty little car and heading away from the building she said, "All right, what's going on?"

"I heard today that I've won the MacKellar Award."

Ginny turned to face him. She couldn't have been more astounded if he'd said he was confirmed on a flight to the moon. The MacKellar Award was given each year for outstanding work in the field of investigative journalism. The award committee was administered by a group of Southern editors and writers. In the South, the award was almost as prestigious as the Pulitzer. "You're kidding!"

"Dead serious."

She felt a wave of intense pride, which shone in her eyes. "Why, Bret, that's wonderful! What story of yours was judged?"

When he didn't immediately answer or meet her eyes, she began to feel uncomfortable. "Bret?"

His gaze flickered over her, then he concentrated on the street before him as he downshifted and turned a corner. "It wasn't one story. It was a series that was published right after you left."

Dread weighed heavily on her heart. "Series? I didn't know you were working on one."

"It was Frank's idea. In fact, he was the one who called me to let me know about the award."

Something clicked in her mind. "Those clippings you had in your office. Was that the series?" She wished now she'd read them, instead of letting her stubbornness get the better of her.

"Yes."

When he offered nothing further she clucked her tongue in exasperation. "Don't make me drag it out of you, Bret."

He glanced over as if to correctly gauge the frustration in her face. "Shortly after you and I were married, Frank had an idea about trying to get an inside story on organized crime in the South. I was the natural choice to do the series. I had some contacts, people who knew I wouldn't use their names if they talked to me."

Ginny's mouth went dry, and she felt as if someone had made a fist around her heart. "That's where you were all those nights you didn't come home."

Bret pulled into the driveway and stopped behind her car. He cut the engine and turned to lean against the door. His head rested against the glass. A street lamp cast light onto his chest and lower body, but left his face in shadow. His voice was as deep and dark as the night, with none of its usual briskness or teasing tones. "Yes. That's where I was. The kind of guys I was talking to don't exactly keep nine-to-five jobs, you know. I had to work when they worked." He snorted derisively. "If extortion, illegal gambling and drug dealing could be called work."

"Why didn't you tell me?"

"Because if something went wrong I didn't want you to be in danger."

"You should have told me," she insisted hotly, leaning across the small console in an attempt to see his face better. "I was your wife!"

"Funny, as I recall, the wedding vows said something about for better or worse. I guess that part wasn't binding."

"Don't you dare throw the blame on me! I had the right to know if your life was at risk." She caught her breath suddenly. "That's the story you were working on the night you were hurt, wasn't it?"

"Yes."

Ginny propped her elbow on the open window and cradled her forehead in her palm. "I had the right to know," she repeated, almost to herself.

"And *I* had the right to protect you from the harm any knowledge might have brought you. As your husband, that was my responsibility."

Ginny sat back and crossed her arms over her chest, matching his pose. They were at an impasse—not their first. It was childish, she knew, but she couldn't help thinking if he'd really wanted her back he would have fought harder for her. Instead, when he *had* come after her, he'd accused her of cowardice and walked away. She had to wonder if he'd considered her too immature to handle the information about the danger he was in. "Why didn't you tell me the truth when you followed me here last February?"

"You seemed determined to stay with Hugh, and he was so sick I knew he needed you. Besides, the threat hadn't passed." He paused, then his next words came in a self-mocking tone. "Also, I was pretty damned mad that you hadn't stuck it out."

Although she was sitting perfectly still, staring down at her hands, Ginny felt as if she'd been picked up and tossed away like a worthless tennis ball. It appeared that some of the assumptions she'd made about Bret were wrong. Others were now confirmed. He'd cared about her in his own way, but his job came first. "Let's face it, Bret, putting everything else aside, you were willing to let me go rather than risk losing a story."

He sat up and wrenched open the car door. "If that's true, Ginny, what am I doing here?"

"Heaven only knows!" Exasperated, Ginny followed his lead, emerging from the car to stand looking at him over its top. "Hiding out?"

His reluctant grin flashed in the streetlight's dim glow. "I think I'll let you stew over that one for a while, Ginny. Good night. I'd see you to your door, but an independent woman like you, who doesn't need any protection, might be offended by the gesture." Flicking his hand in a jaunty salute, he started away, then turned back. "Oh, by the way, the MacKellar Award dinner is a week from Thursday. Would you like to go as my date? No? Well, that's okay, I can find someone.'' He waved again and began to climb the stairs to the garage apartment.

Ginny stood, clenching her fists as she listened to the scuff of his shoes on the stairs and wondering why she felt as if *she* was the one in the wrong.

# CHAPTER FIVE

DORIS! BRET HAD TAKEN Doris to the MacKellar
Award dinner.

Ginny sat in the deserted offices of the *Herald* with
her feet propped on a cardboard box, her hands behind her head and her mind in the same confusion it
had been in since the night of the high-school open
house.

For more than a week she'd speculated about Bret's
date, looking at all the women in the office—in fact,
all the women in town—with curiosity. She had wondered about it, told herself she wasn't the least bit
jealous and been heartily relieved when Doris had
made her happy announcement.

The fact that Bret had invited Doris again showed
how much he'd changed. In his days as a hotshot reporter he hadn't really tried to find out the needs or
problems of his fellow employees. He hadn't been
rude, but merely absorbed in his career, his next story.

Now he'd taken the time to get to know Doris, to
find out she had been the local authority on the
MacKellar Award since the year Hugh had been on the
nominating committee. Bret had also discovered that
Doris dearly loved trips to Columbia, but hated to
drive long distances alone. Since the death of her husband several years earlier, Doris had seldom been farther than Greenville.

Bret's thoughtfulness both pleased and troubled Ginny. She was firmly convinced he wouldn't be staying in Webster. But if he planned to leave, why was he working so hard to improve the paper? For instance, he'd asked her to write articles on the schools, focusing on individual outstanding students, the first of which would appear in next week's issue. She knew they'd be popular.

And why was he going out of his way for the people in town, strangers to him? Not for Sam and Laura's sake. Everyone already knew and liked them. Not for Ginny. She and Bret were divorced and leading separate lives.

Ginny pulled her feet off the box and sat up in disgust. She pushed her nail-bitten fingers through her hair in frustration until the blond strands were as tangled as her thoughts. Her sister's question kept echoing through her mind. What *was* stopping her from getting to know her ex-husband better? What had prevented her from accepting his invitation to go to the dinner and see him accept the award? She had spent the evening before moping around the house, imagining Bret's pleasure at receiving the award, the speech he'd given. She'd also imagined herself sitting in Doris's place, showing the world how proud of him she was.

What was stopping her? The only honest answer was fear. She was afraid of letting him matter too much to her.

Restlessly she got up and wandered around the empty building, making sure things were put away for the weekend and locking up.

Bret and Doris had been gone since the previous morning, a Thursday, and were due back anytime—

not that Ginny expected them to come to the office. The county fair was starting this afternoon and everyone else had left the office early. Doris had entered a quilt in the quilt-making competition, so she would probably go straight to the fairgrounds to see if she'd won. Ginny had no idea what Bret would do. She couldn't believe a simple county fair would hold much attraction for him, especially not after having received the MacKellar Award.

Ginny turned off the lights in the advertising section and closed the door, then moved slowly down the hall to retrieve her purse. She could admit that she felt immense pride at Bret's accomplishment, even though she experienced a bit of professional jealousy, too. She hoped to win it herself someday.

The whole idea of the award deeply troubled her. The dinner would have been attended by the best, brightest and most ambitious editors in the South. She was certain that more than one would have offered Bret a job. They'd have been crazy not to. Hiring a MacKellar winner was a true feather in the cap.

After Bret and Doris had left, Ginny had gone into his office for something and seen the manila envelope full of clippings that Frank Brevard had sent him. She'd filched it without a twinge of conscience and carried it back to her own desk, where she had neglected the piece she was writing on Jeffrey Biggs and read through the articles.

They were wonderful, undoubtedly the best things Bret had ever written, but when she thought of the situations he'd exposed himself to in order to obtain the interviews, her blood ran cold. If she'd known the danger he was in while doing the story, she would have had hysterics—which was probably why Bret hadn't told her where he really was on those nights she'd thought he was out with the vice squad.

Once she'd read the stories, Ginny was more convinced than ever that some editor would offer him a plum position. Bret would be a fool not to accept.

If that happened, Ginny wasn't sure she'd want to return to being the editor of the *Herald*. It was rather pleasant to simply pursue stories assigned to her without worrying about everything from headlines to cost overruns. Besides, if Bret left, she would miss him terribly.

Which was one reason to keep her distance from him. She had survived the hurt of her broken marriage, but wasn't sure she could survive any more such hurts. On the other hand, Bret hadn't really indicated that he wanted her back. She didn't know what she'd do if he did.

Frustrated with her endlessly treadmilling thoughts, she grabbed her purse, locked the front door and drove home. As she parked, she noticed that Bret's car wasn't in its usual place. She was sorry that he wasn't there because she wanted to tell him she'd read the articles and felt he richly deserved the award. Her father greeted her as she came in, dancing lightly toward her. He was freshly showered and shaved, dressed in a good pair of slacks and a new blue shirt. He hooked her purse from her shoulder and hung it on the hall coatrack, then took her hands and twirled her in a waltz.

"Hurry and change your clothes, Ginny girl. There's big doin's at the fairgrounds and I want to take my favorite girl. The seniors' club is holding a dance at the gazebo and I want to see if I remember how to fox-trot. If I do, I'll teach you."

She grinned and hugged him. "Dad, I'd rather dance something a little more contemporary."

He was appalled. "Don't be ridiculous. Those silly boogie dances will be out of fashion by next year. The fox-trot will be with us forever."

She laughed, pleased she'd be spending some time with Hugh, whom she'd hardly seen in the past few weeks. He seemed to be making real progress on his novel, though, shutting himself up in his den for hours on end. Often she could hear him typing late into the night. He was definitely preoccupied and would only say that his writing was going well. He hadn't even given her a hint of the plot or characters. And, while she hadn't been able to convince him to go in for a checkup, his health seemed to have improved. He hadn't coughed in that frightening way in more than two weeks.

Oh, yes, it would be wonderful to spend the evening with him. She wouldn't miss Bret at all. Ginny was proud of herself for not asking if Hugh had seen Bret that day.

She hurried upstairs to change into jeans, a long-sleeved shirt and sneakers. Knowing the evening would turn chilly once the sun was down, she tied the sleeves of a delft-blue sweater around her shoulders, then brushed her hair and rushed back downstairs.

THE FAIRGROUNDS were already crowded by the time they arrived. Lines to buy tickets for the rides snaked away from the ticket booths for a hundred feet or more.

Hugh looked at the patiently waiting customers and grinned. "It's probably just as well. My days of taking you on those spine-busting monsters are long gone.''

"Dad, you never took me on those rides!" she protested. "Mom did, and I was the one who took Carrie."

"Well, it's obviously too late for me to start now," he said with fervent gratitude, taking her arm and heading for the exhibition buildings.

Ginny loved the annual fair. There were booths along open walkways that sold everything from popcorn and lemonade to slices of homemade pie. As well, community groups sponsored games of chance to raise money for their programs; she promised herself to come back later and try her hand at some of them.

The county fair may have seemed hokey to some, but to her it was an important part of the community and one of the things she liked about living in the same small town in which she'd grown up. It was nice to greet people she'd known all her life as she walked along the wide graveled path, her arm linked with her father's.

In the livestock building Hugh met a group of friends and stopped to chat. Uninterested in comparing the merits of one type of cattle feed with another, Ginny wandered over to the area where domestic accomplishments were displayed. She discovered that Doris's wedding-ring quilt, done in bright primary shades, had won a blue ribbon. She didn't know if Doris had arrived yet, but she hoped her friend would be there soon to enjoy the award.

After she'd admired the quilt, Ginny headed out to the midway where barkers invited the crowd, mostly children, to try the "death-defying" rides. She walked past them and went back to the booths sponsored by local groups.

Her steps slowed when she neared the dunking booth being run by the Webster Boosters Club. The couple in charge of it were her dentist and his wife. She waved to them and stopped to watch. A big tank of the type used to water cattle was filled to the brim, and a board was balanced over it. A volunteer sat on the board, while people in the crowd paid for the chance to throw a softball at the metal disk attached to a lever on the side of the tank. A hit tipped the person on the board into the water.

Sam Calhoun was standing before the booth with a decidedly satisfied expression on his face. The sheriff, Farley Hunkle, was just surfacing from a dunking, slicking his wispy hair away from his pinched wet face.

"You shouldn't have given me that parking ticket, Farley," Sam said, a huge grin on his face.

"You deserved it, Sam," Farley grumbled as he grasped the sides of a wooden ladder and hauled himself out of the tank, then squished his way to a small tent set up as a changing room.

Ginny heard a snicker behind her and turned to see her former sister-in-law. Laura Calhoun was sitting on a bench, leaning back awkwardly on one hand, apparently trying to find a position that would accommodate the swell of her stomach and still be comfortable. Ginny had always been grateful that Sam and Laura had not blamed her for the divorce, but had treated her with kindness and sympathy whenever they saw her.

"How are you feeling?" Ginny asked, moving closer to Laura.

With a wave, Laura invited her to sit down. "As if I'm about to give birth to an elephant. Although I'm beginning to doubt that I'll ever give birth," she answered with a sigh, but her eyes glowed with happiness.

Ginny smiled even as she felt a twinge of envy. "When are you due?"

"Four more weeks."

Despite the tiredness evident in her face, Laura was nothing short of beautiful. Her once short strawberry-blond hair had been allowed to grow so that it fell in soft curls just below the collar of her apricot-colored maternity top.

"Feeling pretty rough?"

"My own mother says I'm the largest pregnant woman she's ever seen. Since she's had six of her own, she should know what she's talking about."

"I guess so. I'm surprised to see you here. How's the ankle?"

"My ankle?"

"The one you sprained a few weeks ago."

Frowning in puzzlement, Laura shook her head. "I twisted my ankle a little while ago when I was dragging one of Sam's silly dogs out of my roses, but it was fine in a day or so."

"Oh. I thought it was more severe," Ginny murmured. "I'm glad you're better." Although her smile was warm, inwardly she was seething. Her father had tricked her, and she'd bet big money that Bret was in on it, too. Bret surely would have known that Laura's ankle injury wasn't as debilitating as Hugh had indicated. He hadn't bothered to tell her, though. Just wait until she saw those two men again!

"Hasn't given me another twinge—Uh-oh."

Alarmed, Ginny reached for her. "What's the matter? Are you in pain?"

"No, but look." She nodded toward the booth.

Ginny turned around to see Bret scooting carefully out onto the board above the tank. He was dressed in jeans and an old blue T-shirt that had Vanderbilt University printed across the front in faded letters. Ginny remembered that it was the shirt he'd always worn while washing his truck. Obviously he'd come home after she and Hugh had left.

Ginny watched with growing interest as he positioned himself on the board. He looked assessingly at his brother, then smiled.

"Sam, you got lucky with that last pitch."

"In your dreams, little brother. I wasn't even in top form." Sam reached into the metal bucket full of baseballs, pulled one out and rubbed it gleefully, as Bret chuckled.

The man in charge of the booth went into a spiel designed to attract customers. "Take your best shot at the new editor of the *Herald*," he invited the crowd. "Has he misspelled your name? Printed your ad wrong? Told the whole town you actually like your mother-in-law? Here's your chance for revenge!"

The two women laughed, then Laura propped her forearm on the swell of her stomach and said thoughtfully, "You know, Ginny, there's nothing really *wrong* with the Calhoun men. They're just bullheaded and stubborn. And they think they know what's best for everyone else."

"I'm aware of that," Ginny said. "They also keep important information to themselves, if they think it'll serve their own ends." She was thinking of Laura's ankle.

"That's true. In fact, I've always secretly believed they were throwbacks to the caveman era. They see the woman they want and drag her home with them whether she wants to go or not."

"A pretty old-fashioned bunch."

"A smart woman wouldn't miss a chance to take them down a peg or two."

"I was always at the top of my class in school," Ginny said modestly, her eyes sparkling with mischief.

"I'd say you were pretty smart, then." Laura nodded toward the tank. "How many times in her life does a woman get a chance like this?"

"Not many. In fact, this may be my only one. There's no one in line behind Sam, so I could take my chance right now."

Without another word, Ginny stood, and helped Laura to her feet. Laura walked over to her husband and manufactured an air of gentle suffering. "Sam, I'm tired. I'd like to go home."

Immediately Sam dropped the softball he'd been handling into the metal bucket and reached for his wife. He swiftly ran his hands over her face and shoulders, then checked her pulse. "What's wrong? Are you having pains? I told you we shouldn't have come." He barely spared Ginny a glance as he fussed. "Hi, Ginny, how's it going?"

Ginny didn't even bother to answer, since he obviously wasn't listening.

As Sam took a firm grip on his wife and began to lead her away, Laura rolled her eyes and said, "Good luck. I'd stay and watch, but it looks as if I'm about to be taken home and pampered, and that's something I don't want to miss."

Ginny waved and grinned, then dug in her purse for some money. She laid a five-dollar bill on the table with exaggerated care. "This entitles me to five shots, Sally," she told the woman running the booth. "And if I miss, there's plenty more where that came from, because today was payday."

She removed her sweater and handed it and her purse to Sally to stash under the table, then turned happily to face Bret.

He slowly swung his head from side to side, his eyes wary. "Uh, Ginny, you really don't want to do this."

She leaned over the bucket and pulled out a ball. "Oh, yes, I do." Her blue eyes held only innocence. "By the way, how was the award dinner?"

"Fine, fine." Bret clasped the edge of the board. "You know, this is no way to treat the winner of the MacKellar."

"Maybe not, but there's something about a sitting duck that I just can't resist."

"You're not actually going to try to dunk me, are you?"

"Oh, no, I won't try."

His fingers relaxed slightly.

"I'll succeed."

He gripped the board again. "I never knew you had a cruel streak in you."

"You learn something new every day."

He laughed, then sobered as she began to lob the ball from one hand to the other. Someone called out to her from the gathering crowd, and she turned to toss the ball to him. This continued for a couple of minutes as she warmed up her arm.

"Uh, Ginny?" Bret called out. "I just remembered something."

"What's that?"

"You played on Sam's softball team, didn't you?"

"How clever of you to remember."

"Do you mind if I ask what position you played?"

"Not at all." She braced her feet, leaned forward and studied the distance to the metal disk, then glanced up. "I was the pitcher." With that, she rocked back, lifted her left knee to give herself better balance and put everything she had behind the throw. Since she usually threw underhand, she was a little off, and the ball missed the disk by scant millimeters.

"Need glasses?" Bret jeered, but she held up her hand as calmly superior as a duchess and selected another ball. She took aim and let the ball fly. It hit the target. Lights flashed, whistles blew and Bret plunged into the water.

Behind her there was a smattering of applause. Ginny turned and bowed, accepting the admiration of those who had come to watch. She heard splashing behind her and looked back to see Bret, who, instead of heading for the ladder that would take him out of the tank near the tent, was coming straight for her. She squeaked in alarm as he slithered over the side of the tank and sloshed his way to her, wincing slightly as gravel bit into his bare feet.

Ginny started stuttering as she backed away. "N-now, B-Bret..."

"I think maybe they forgot to mention something about this booth." He wiped water off his face.

"What's that?"

"That if the dunker succeeds in dunking the dunkee, the dunkee gets to kiss the dunker."

It took her several seconds to sort through his convoluted sentence, but when she got his meaning she gasped. "Farley didn't kiss Sam."

"Ginny, Sam's my brother, but even *I* wouldn't want to kiss him."

She glanced at the interested faces around her, but saw only amusement. No help there. "I won't do it."

"Well, there's always the forfeit. You can spend the evening with me here at the fair."

"I think you're making this up."

"Are you afraid?"

"Certainly not!" But she couldn't look him in the eye. Instead, she took in the sight of the T-shirt plastered to his chest and the jeans that appeared to have been spray-painted on.

He grinned when she blushed.

"Then you'll do it? Spend the evening with me?"

"Oh, all right." Her answer was less than gracious, but it didn't seem to matter to Bret.

"Wait right here. I'll be back." He turned and walked toward the dressing tent. Ginny saw more than one woman watch his progress, then examine her with envy. She sighed as she wondered what she'd gotten herself into. If she was smart, she'd spend the wait reinforcing her defenses. She walked over to retrieve her purse and sweater, figuring she had fifteen minutes before Bret returned.

He was back in ten, with his hair combed, though still damp. He was dressed in dry jeans and a cinnamon-colored pullover, carrying his wet clothes in a plastic bag. As if he knew the doubts she was having, he took her arm and led her toward the rides.

"Those lines for tickets are a mile long," she said in a last desperate attempt to discourage him.

"Not to worry." He dug into his pocket and produced a flattened roll of tickets. "I paid that kid who lives next door, Jimmy Blaines, to stand in line and buy these for me. He brought them to the dunking booth."

"You think of everything."

"I try," he answered with a not-so-modest smirk. "Let's go put my wet clothes and your purse in my car."

"My purse?" She clutched the big hobo bag to her chest.

"Honey, everything you own is in that purse. It weighs more than you do. If you drop it while we're on one of these rides, you might kill someone standing beneath us."

"It's not heavy," she murmured. But knowing she had lost the argument, she followed him out to the Geo to lock their belongings inside. The sun had set and the parking area was poorly lit. When Ginny stumbled over a rock, Bret put his arm around her and left it there. She knew she should pull away once they reached the glaring lights of the midway, but felt content to stay right where she was, with her own arm around his waist.

He led her into a line crowded with dozens of kids waiting for a ride that was shaped like a giant wheel of fortune. The riders sat two to a cage and were held in by a heavy metal bar across their laps. As it spun faster and faster, the wheel rose on one side until it was almost vertical. The lights on the outside whirled in a dazzling display of color. Ginny blinked.

"Losing your courage?"

"You'd love to tease me if I was, but I'm not." She grinned at him. "But did you notice that we're the only people in this line who are over the age of fifteen?"

"What difference does that make? Unless you *are* afraid?"

"Of course not!" she exclaimed, then narrowed her eyes in warning when he grinned at her. He knew she couldn't resist a dare.

As they waited, she realized with a slight sense of shock that she was happy. She couldn't think of a better place for her to be alone with Bret. There were people everywhere, many of whom she knew. She could spend the evening with Bret, enjoying his sense of humor and fun, without being overwhelmed by memories—or by his intense masculinity. When she was ready to leave, all she had to do was find her father. Why had she been so worried? Things would work out just fine.

It was starting to cool off, so she untied her sweater from around her neck and put it on. She adjusted the sleeves and reached up to pull her hair out of the collar, but Bret did it first.

Hands suspended in midair, she met his gaze. He smiled, slowly and sweetly, as if his gesture was perfectly innocent.

His fingertips slid against the base of her neck, sending shivers downward from the point of contact. The shivers moved inward, bringing everything inside her to life. Alarm bells rang in her mind. "Bret?"

"Don't worry, honey. What can I possibly do in a crowd like this?"

That had been her thought exactly, but now she knew. He could rob her of her defenses with his slightest touch. She didn't have time to answer, though, because the giant wheel had stopped, the riders were departing, and the line was moving forward.

She would have run away, but he guided her forward into a cage that had the queen of hearts painted on the outside. She slid across the worn vinyl seats, and Bret followed, fastening the bar across their laps. The attendant came by to make sure the bar was secure, then moved on.

"You don't get seasick, do you?"

Ginny, finally getting into the spirit of things, gave him a disbelieving stare. "Of course not. We used to have a water bed, remember?"

Bret nearly choked on her bawdy remark and was laughing as the ride started. Within seconds they were spinning around, which caused her to slam up against him, tighter than paint on plaster. She tried to put her arm between them and scoot away on the slippery seat, but to no avail. The next turn of the wheel had him slamming against her.

Through the roaring of the motor and the rush of wind, he shouted into her ear, "Give it up, Ginny. We're going to be stuck together like glue until this is over. Might as well enjoy it." She nodded as they were snapped forward once again, nearly separating her head from her spine.

In spite of the centrifugal forces that had them pressed against the seat and each other, he managed to lift his arm and put it around her. She snuggled close to him, telling herself she was doing so to keep her head braced.

They whirled in what seemed like every direction of the compass at once. When the wheel lifted into its vertical position, she pried her eyelids open long enough to see the ground and then the lighted sky spin past. She shrieked and shut her eyes again. Bret's chuckle bounced her head against his chest, and she pinched him just above the waistband of his jeans. He yelped and retaliated by putting his thumb under her chin, lifting her face and lowering his mouth to cover hers.

At first, Ginny was too stunned to react, then was too enthralled to draw away. The tumbling sensations that shot through her duplicated the wild spinning of their bodies.

His lips were warm and firm, exactly as she remembered them, only more exciting. Her addled brain couldn't remember if he'd ever affected her this way before. He must have, though, because he was so intense and never did anything with less than his best effort. Finally she just gave up trying to figure anything out and kissed him back. Each kiss was a long drugging exploration of taste and texture that barely ended before the next began. It was wonderful and terrifying and, oh, so familiar.

The ride began to slow and descend, bringing them easily down to earth. Bret kept right on kissing her. He obviously had no intention of bringing *her* down easily. He had stolen her breath and reason and tucked them away somewhere. Ginny suspected he intended to keep them so she'd be permanently off balance—or out of her mind.

He was still kissing the daylights out of her when the attendant came by to unhook the bar holding them in. Finally Bret let her up for air, and she blinked as if she'd just wandered out of a dark cave.

The attendant was grinning down at them, his eyes full of admiration. "Buddy, that's the first time I ever saw anybody hold a liplock like that when the wheel was at full speed."

"Beginner's luck," Bret said smoothly as he stepped out and lifted Ginny to her feet. She was so muddled she thought her knees would have bent backward if Bret hadn't been there to hold her up. He had them off the platform and down the steps before her brain began to function normally.

"Bret, stop!" she insisted, as he hurried her to the next ride. "I don't want to go on any more rides with you."

He managed to appear hurt in spite of the devilment gleaming in his eyes. "Ah, come on, Ginny. I've already bought all these tickets. It would be a shame to let them go to waste."

"You could give them away!" But her protests did no good. He hustled her onto another gravity-defying contraption. Looking like a bunch of huge seashells with seats, it apparently had the sole purpose of keeping her in Bret's lap as it shuttled rapidly back and forth across a surface that resembled a shallow bowl.

He kept his lips to himself on that one, and she didn't know whether to be relieved or disappointed—which told her exactly what effect Bret was having on her. Spending the evening with him had been a truly bad idea, she decided, as he grabbed her hand and dragged her to the next ride with all the fervor of a man on the verge of making a gold strike. And she'd tell him just how bad an idea this had been, as soon as they got off this darned Ferris wheel.

She knew she wouldn't, though, because they were having too much fun. From the top of the wheel, they gazed out over the fairgrounds, enjoying the view. As they whooshed downward, Ginny caught sight of her father deep in conversation with Jimmy Blaines. She waved, but he didn't see her because his back was to her. She saw him throw his hands in the air and wondered if Jimmy was once again trying to raise the price of the worms he caught for Hugh. When she and Bret disembarked from the wheel, Hugh had disappeared.

When they ran out of tickets, they tried several games of chance. Bret won her a stuffed panda almost as big as she was and made her carry it herself. So she retaliated by making him hold it while she lingered in the women's room.

He dared her to go into the hall of mirrors with him, then laughed when she found a mirror that made her seem inches taller and pounds thinner and vowed she was going to take it home with her. He promised to buy her one just like it. By the time they stumbled back out into the crowd, they were both parched and hungry. Though it was nearly nine o'clock at night, he bought hot dogs and sodas, and they sat down at a table, utterly exhausted. Ginny hadn't been this content in months.

They were finishing their snack when Hugh walked up. He seemed quite satisfied about something, although he greeted Ginny with a mild admonition. "Did you forget about the dance you promised me, honey?"

Horrified, she clapped a hand to her forehead. "Oh, Dad, I'm sorry." The truth was that she had forgotten about everything in the world except Bret. "Are you tired, Dad? Do you want to go dance now? Or we could simply go home. . . ."

Across from her she saw Bret draw back and watch her speculatively as she half rose to fuss over her father. Hugh shook his head. "No, no. I'm okay, but I am going home. I've seen all I want to see and they're going to be closing this place down in another hour. Bret can bring you home.''

Ginny returned to reality in one swift cruel second. She had done exactly what she'd promised herself she wouldn't—gotten too close to Bret. He must be some kind of magician, casting a spell on her. To be fair, she had to admit he hadn't forced her to fall under that spell; she'd managed it all on her own.

"No, I'll come with you, Dad. You might need me.'' Quickly she gathered the napkins and paper cups and chucked them into a trash can. Suddenly Bret was behind her.

"I knew it was too good to last,'' he commented, his gray eyes steady in the glare of the fairground lights.

"What?'' She tucked her hair behind her ears and made herself face him.

"A full evening with you that didn't include recriminations, evasions and worries.''

"I don't—''

"Your purse is in my car, remember? Why don't you let me take you home?''

For some reason she thought he was gravely disappointed in her, but she couldn't fathom why. She shook her head as confusion swamped her. "Just leave it. I'll get it tomorrow.'' She turned toward her father who was watching them with ill-concealed interest. "Ready to go, Dad?''

Out of the corner of her eye, she caught a signal between her father and her ex-husband, but before she could decipher it, Bret said, "I'll see you tomorrow, then, Ginny. Good night.''

She took her father's arm and hurried away, but she knew Bret followed her with his eyes until they were out of sight.

Once they were settled in Hugh's car and had driven away from the fairgrounds, Hugh said casually, "You know, I've been thinking."

"About what?" she asked vaguely, her mind still on the evening she'd just shared with Bret, the emotions she'd felt—and the kiss. Oh, dear heaven, that kiss!

"I think I need to be alone to write my novel. There are too many distractions here. Dave Mintnor told me about a cabin in the woods owned by a friend of his. I'm going to rent it."

# CHAPTER SIX

"I WOULDN'T SAY this cabin is exactly remote, but I've seen pictures of foreign-legion outposts with closer neighbors." Her heart sinking, Ginny dug her heel into the soft pine needles that covered the ground and turned slowly. She surveyed the woods edging the small lake beside the cabin her father had rented for the next few months. Other cabins stood on the shore, but they all seemed deserted. The summer season was past and few people remained through the winter.

The place was certainly beautiful, but she chewed her bottom lip worriedly as she regarded the towering trees and the thick undergrowth that would soon be dried and shriveled back by cold weather. Who knew what kind of creatures lurked in the tall grasses? "And don't you think those trees and bushes have a sinister look about them?" she said to Bret. "You know, like the ones in *The Wizard of Oz?*"

"You're exaggerating." He lifted the last box of Hugh's things from the back of his Geo and slammed the hatch. It had taken two cars to bring all the things Ginny had thought her father would need. The three of them had already staggered up the stairs with enough food for six people to survive a month-long blizzard.

Bret glanced around at the trees. "Hey, now you know how I feel living in that god-awful woodland bower."

"It's not god-awful," she said, automatically defending the art teacher's work. "It's much more cheerful than this."

"Do you think the big bad wolf is going to lunge out of the woods and carry your daddy off?" He wiggled his eyebrows at her suggestively. "You should be more worried about yourself. It's a long drive back to Webster and we'll be *all* alone."

Ordinarily she would have had a smart retort, but right now she was worried about Hugh. It had been a full week since the county fair. In that time she had alternately cajoled, begged and sulked—all in vain. She had even called Carrie and enlisted her aid in the attempt to convince their father he could work perfectly well at home. Carrie had come home for the weekend, listened carefully to both sides and then agreed with their father, much to Ginny's dismay. Ginny had argued that since she was gone every day, Hugh had the house to himself and his time was his own.

Hugh's response had been that he needed to be by himself in order to create. The first couple of chapters were coming together, but he wanted to be completely free of distractions, in the evenings, as well, in order to let the rest flow.

Ginny, who had never heard her father talk like that before, didn't know what to make of it. She'd finally concluded that writing fiction was much different than writing for a newspaper. She wished him well, but wanted him closer.

She had to admit the cabin itself wasn't bad. The main living area had a big fireplace and an open kitchen. Above it was a loft bedroom and bathroom. There was plenty of space for one person. The interior was paneled in knotty pine and decorated with rag rugs and heavy Early American furniture that looked as if it had sat stoically through the sixties, seventies and eighties without much wear. Hugh had more than enough food, and Ginny had insisted he buy a cellular phone so she could keep in contact with him. A huge woodpile outside assured her he wouldn't freeze before spring. Still, she was uneasy.

Bret must have seen the anxiety on her face as she gazed at the rustic cabin. He shifted the box to hold it under one arm and moved close enough to put his other arm around her shoulders. He gave her a light friendly squeeze, but his expression was serious. "Ginny, he's a big boy now and you're not responsible for him."

She drew away haughtily and blew her bangs out of her eyes. "Well, of course not! I never said I was."

He gave her a slow smile, making her aware that he was laughing at her even as he sympathized. "Ginny, it's so obvious, you don't *have* to say it."

She stalked toward the cabin. "I'm going inside." She went up the steps and reached for the door just as Hugh swung it open from the inside. She stopped in surprise.

"In a hurry, honey?" Hugh shot a look at Bret, who was climbing the stairs behind her.

"No. I was going in to organize the things in the kitchen for you."

"You don't have to do that."

"I want to, Dad." She opened the door and moved around him.

"Well, don't be too long." Hugh glanced out at the lengthening shadows. "It'll be night before you know it."

"And we have to be on our way," Bret put in, following her to the kitchen. "I'll help you with this."

Hugh paused in the doorway, his attention seemingly caught by the glint of setting sun on the lake's surface. "I think I'll do a bit of exploring down by the lake."

"Okay, Dad." Ginny bit back the urge to remind him to be careful, not wanting to give Bret more reason to chide her. She set to work unpacking the cardboard cartons full of the food she'd painstakingly selected at the supermarket in Webster.

Maybe Bret was right, she thought, as she placed milk and eggs on the refrigerator shelves. There was a slight chance she'd overdone it. Her soft mouth twisted into a grimace as she realized she'd bought enough eggs and milk for Hugh to have a three-egg omelet for breakfast and a custard pie for lunch every day for two weeks. The amount of vegetables and canned goods in the boxes could feed a family of four for at least that long.

She was willing to admit that perhaps she was unnecessarily worried about Hugh. He hadn't had a coughing spell in days and he really seemed excited about being on his own. The problem was that she wasn't sure how she felt about being on *her* own, living in that big empty house with Bret right next door.

Bret was busy loading tins into the cupboards. Ginny gave him a sidelong glance, noticing the ease with which he could pick up two cans of soup with one hand. He had one box emptied, the cans lined up neatly, their labels turned outward, long before she had put all the perishables into the refrigerator. Everything he did was efficient, though recently he seemed to move at half the speed he'd used when they were married. He still accomplished everything that needed to be done, but he did it at a stroll rather than a run.

She was amazed by the changes in him and honestly didn't know what to think of them. The man she'd married wouldn't have been so willing to go out of his way to help someone unless the person was a blood relative or could somehow benefit his career. Bret didn't seem that concerned about his career anymore, though. She knew for a fact that he'd received more than one call from editors following up on the MacKellar Award. Doris had kept her posted.

But Bret didn't seem interested. He appeared content to continue as editor of the *Herald*. Did that mean all her assumptions were wrong? That he wasn't going to pack up any day now and head back to the city?

If he did she would certainly miss him, but in a way she wished he'd go. Ever since their evening at the county fair she'd been far too aware of him. It was as if being close to him, being kissed by him, had chiseled away a tiny section of the wall she'd built around her feelings for him. If she wasn't careful, that wall would crumble into nothingness.

He turned suddenly and caught her standing and staring at him, her hands full of lettuce and carrots, her face full of wonder. His lopsided smile asked her what she'd been thinking about. She was sure her blush told him.

Fortunately he appeared willing to pretend he couldn't read what was on her face. "You don't have to worry about him, Ginny. He'll be fine."

"I...I guess you're right." Quickly she turned to finish her job. When she straightened and shut the refrigerator door, she saw that Bret was leaning against the counter with his arms crossed over his chest and his eyes thoughtful.

"Remember when we used to work together in the kitchen of our apartment?" His voice was quiet, almost dreamy.

Ginny didn't want to remember. She picked up the dishcloth and began wiping the spotless counter in erratic little circles. "You were usually gone, so it didn't happen very often."

"A good thing, too," he answered, moving ever so slightly to block her nervous journey down the counter. She looked up warily when she realized he wasn't going to let her by. His smile was sly and knowing as he continued, "Whenever we were both there, we'd bump into each other, apologize, kiss and end up in the bedroom making love."

She nearly choked as unwanted images crowded into her mind. "Bret...I don't want you to talk about that."

"Afraid?"

"Bored."

He began to laugh just as her father returned. Hugh removed his shoes and set them behind a chair, then wiped his hands on a big handkerchief. "Danged mud," he muttered, looking from her to Bret. Ginny was sure he'd notice the color in her cheeks and the amusement in Bret's eyes, but he didn't comment. "Thick as molasses on that shore."

Glad for a distraction, Ginny held out her hand. "I'll put that in the laundry hamper for you, Dad."

"No, no." He quickly stuffed the handkerchief into his pocket. "I'll do it later. Besides, you don't have to wait on me." He tilted his head toward the window where the sun was sinking fast. "You'd better head home. From the looks of that sky, I think it might rain."

This was the moment Ginny had been dreading. Not only would she miss her father, she'd be living alone for the first time in her life. She had gone from a big house busy with the activities of three people to a college dormitory ringing with noise and laughter, and then married a man whose very presence had seemed to fill every corner of their apartment even when he wasn't there.

Hugh reached out to shake hands with Bret. "Take care of my little girl and my newspaper, Bret. I know I can trust you with both."

Bret gave the older man a sharp glance. Hugh met his eyes squarely. Ginny sensed some kind of silent communication between them, but she didn't know what it could be about. Bret grinned suddenly and pumped Hugh's hand with enthusiasm. "Yes, sir. You can definitely trust me."

Bret seemed happy as he turned toward the door. "I'll wait for you outside, Ginny."

Hugh sighed in apparent contentment. It seemed as if the two men had struck a bargain. Ginny hoped it had nothing to do with her, but she wasn't that naive.

"Dad, you're not really expecting him to look out for me, are you?"

The picture of innocence, he shrugged as if to ask how she could think such a thing of him. "Of course not, honey. I know you're a grown woman. You have a career, friends. Why, with me out of the way, you can even start dating. I hear Joe Franklin is single again.''

Ginny rolled her eyes. "Dad, I'm not interested in one of your former pressmen, a guy who's thirty, looks fifty, acts twenty, can't hold a job and just dumped wife number three.''

"Pity.'' He sighed, but his eyes were teasing as he pulled her into a hug. She wrapped her arms around his waist and rested her head on his shoulder. For the past several months, she had taken care of him, and now he held her tenderly and told her how much he would miss her.

Ginny stayed where she was with her eyes closed, remembering what it had been like, years ago, before her mother had died. She'd only been a little girl then, without any responsibilities. She realized with a sense of shock, that, by moving out, her father was trying to give some of that back to her. She stepped away and said, "I love you, Dad. I guess we'll see you for Thanksgiving?'' That wouldn't be too bad, she thought. The holiday was just over a month away.

"Count on it.'' He walked her outside to the car, held the door for her and shut it behind her. As Bret drove off, Ginny twisted in her seat to wave to Hugh, who stood on the cabin steps, grinning.

"He'll be all right, Ginny,'' Bret said, glancing over to see the yearning in her face.

"I know.''

"And so will you.''

She smiled tremulously, but didn't answer. Instead, she faced front as the sporty little car bounced along the rutted private drive that led out to a dirt road.

They would travel on the graded road for ten miles, then turn onto the highway that would take them back to Webster, fifty miles away.

Night was falling and dark clouds rolled in from the east. Ginny knew she should have been more concerned about Hugh, but somehow Bret's reassurances had helped. She felt content and curiously light-hearted knowing that she was going to have a measure of freedom she'd never experienced before. She leaned her head back and watched the shadows of the pines move past as Bret gripped the wheel and guided the car over the rough road. Feeling tired yet satisfied, she settled into the plush seat and let her attention drift to the man beside her.

Bret was still a puzzle to her, but one she was more and more willing to solve. When Carrie had been home the previous weekend, they'd indulged in a long session of girl talk. Carrie had played devil's advocate, asking Ginny what would be the worst thing that could happen if she got close to Bret once more.

Ginny had already known the answer. The worst that could happen would be falling in love with him again.

When they had driven about six miles, Bret straightened with a grunt of surprise, his eyes on a red light glowing on the dashboard. "Son of a gun," he muttered, easing to the side of the road.

"What's wrong?" Ginny sat up sleepily.

"The radiator light's on." Bret took a flashlight from the glove compartment and went out to check under the hood.

Ginny followed him into the early-evening gloom, and the two of them stood with their heads together looking at the engine. Shining the beam of light over it, Bret cursed softly. "Darn. The radiator hose is broken."

"Oh, no." Ginny shivered as she nervously glanced around. "What do we do now?"

He leaned on one elbow, demonic amusement gleaming in his eyes. "Take off your clothes."

*"What?"*

Bret aimed the flashlight at her shoes. "Are you wearing panty hose?"

"Bret, when did you go crazy?"

"Just answer the question," he insisted, moving the beam upward until she was blinded.

"No, I'm not wearing panty hose," she said, batting the flashlight away. "No woman in her right mind would wear panty hose under jeans."

"Darn again." He shook his head and went back to staring at the radiator.

Ginny waited and, when he didn't explain, tapped him on the shoulder. "Well?"

"Well, what?"

"Why did you ask me that?"

He turned toward her and she could see his grin in the faint light. "'Cause I wanted to see how bold you'd be out here in the middle of nowhere?"

"I don't believe that." She tried to sound huffy, but her lips twitched, giving her away.

"All right, I'll confess. I read somewhere that you can temporarily mend a break in a car hose by wrapping a woman's nylon stocking around it."

She gave him a skeptical look. "Did you intentionally break the hose so you could test your theory?"

"Of course not. I'm not *that* desperate to be alone with you."

Ginny made a face at him.

Ignoring her, he slammed the hood down. "This thing's not going anywhere. Come on, it's only about four miles to the highway."

"We're going to walk?" Ginny looked around at the trees, which seemed to become more sinister with each passing minute.

"Unless you'd rather wait for me here?" He stood with the car door open as he studied her over its top. "Don't worry. I'll protect you from the wild animals." The car's interior light illuminated his chin and the straight line of his nose, but left the rest of his face in shadow, giving him a truly devilish appearance.

Yes, but who would protect her from him? Ginny had that fleeting thought as he closed his door and pocketed the keys. She knew she was being silly; they would be safer together. There was no telling when someone might drive by on this road, and while she wanted help she didn't want to be alone to accept it. "Better the devil you know than the devil you don't," she mumbled to herself.

"What?"

"Oh, nothing. Nothing."

"Come on, then," he said, grasping her hand. "It'll take us an hour or so, but we can do it. You never know, we might find a cabin that has a phone."

Pleased by the knowledge he had a plan in mind, as well as by his protectiveness, Ginny grabbed her bag from the front seat and allowed herself to be led away from the dubious safety of the car. They had gone a hundred yards down the road when a gust of wind sent shivers through her. "I forgot my jacket," she said, taking the flashlight from his hand. "If you give me the keys, I'll go back for it."

He handed them to her. "I can get it—"

"No, no. It'll only take a second." She hurried back the way they'd come, unlocked the car and leaned in to grab her denim jacket. Anxious to return to Bret, she pulled it on, settled her bag on her shoulder once again, hit the lock, slammed the door and ran down the road to Bret.

"All set?" He took the light, shone it over her, then smiled as he reached up to pull her collar out and straighten it.

Touched by his gesture, Ginny smiled. "Yes, although if we walk fast, I may be *too* warm."

"Not much chance of that. I just felt a drop of rain."

"You're kidding." Ginny looked up at the sky she couldn't see, and a drop hit her eye. "You're not kidding." Her voice went flat with discouragement. This had not been the best of days, or weeks, and she was feeling the strain. Shoulders slumping, she squinted at him through the darkness. Within seconds, the rain had become a steady drizzle. "Now what?"

"Our plans have changed. Maybe we'd better wait in the car, at least until this lets up."

Ginny sighed as they turned back. She couldn't think of anything worse than being cooped up in that tiny space with him—except maybe being cooped up there alone.

When they reached the car, Bret held out his hand. "Give me the keys."

She blinked at him. "I already gave them back to you."

He patted the pockets of his slacks and windbreaker. "No, you didn't."

She started searching through her purse. "Of course I did."

"If you put them in your bag, we'll be looking for them all night," he groused. As she dug, he shone the flashlight into the car's interior. "Look." The keys glinted brightly from the front seat. Ginny must have dropped them there when she'd grabbed her jacket. Mouth set, he regarded her steadily.

Ginny met his angry eyes in sheepish acknowledgment and lifted her hands helplessly. "Oops."

Obviously fighting for control, Bret clapped his hand over the bottom portion of his face, then drew it down slowly, revealing a formidable expression. Then he stood straight and stiff, towering over her. "I'm a remarkably patient man, Ginny."

"And believe me, I'm grateful for that," she answered fervently. For no good reason her emotions had gone from discomfort to shame to hilarity. Hysterical giggles threatened to explode from her, but she didn't have the nerve to let them surface. Instead, she gulped them back and wiped rainwater from her solemn face.

Bret put his hands on his hips and rocked onto his toes. Even before he spoke, she knew his fury was mounting. "Most men wouldn't be understanding if they were stranded by the side of the road in the rain after their wife had locked the keys in the car."

"Yes, but I'm not your wife."

"Too bad." His tone was level as he brushed rainwet hair from his eyes. "Some juries would consider throttling you quite justifiable."

"You wouldn't want to do that. Think how it would upset my Dad and Carrie, and you like them, don't you?"

"Much more than I like you at this moment."

"I'm sorry to hear that, Bret." She tried to sound mournful. It wasn't hard. The giggles had died as their true situation penetrated along with the rain. They were quiet then, as the rain drizzled down on them, drenching their faces, hair and shoulders. Ginny shivered. "Bret?"

"Yes?" The last consonant hissed into the darkness.

"What do we do now?"

"I don't know."

"You could break a window and unlock the door."

He looked as if she'd suggested murder.

"Bret, it's only a car."

"It's brand-new."

She gave up the argument, took the flashlight and leaned close to examine the lock. "Couldn't you jimmy this?"

His temper made an almost audible snap. "Ginny, I'm a newspaper editor, not a lock picker."

"It was just a suggestion!"

"A bad one!"

"Well, then, you think of something."

"I will!"

"Good!"

Their shouting match was followed by long moments of silence during which Ginny patiently endured the rain soaking through her clothes. She sneezed, then glared at him with great dignity. "Have you thought of a plan yet?"

Clearly unhappy, he took the flashlight from her and said, "We do what we started out to do," he growled. "We walk." He turned, put his arm around her shoulders and started off once again. She tried to keep distance between them, but he wouldn't allow it, pulling her against his hip. "Don't even think it, Ginny. I don't want you falling in the mud."

"You're so thoughtful." She answered through clenched teeth because she knew if she talked normally they'd clatter together like castanets. Even as she thought about how miserably cold she was, the drizzle increased to a steady rain. Ginny began to shiver.

"The faster we walk, the warmer we'll be."

She didn't see how that was possible since she was slowly freezing from the top down. But she simply nodded and lowered her head as they continued to walk through the downpour. Bret had to be as miserable as she was, but he wasn't complaining. Of course if he'd been willing to break into his car, they wouldn't be in this fix.

They increased their pace, desperately hoping a car would come. None did, and the rain was quickly turning the dirt road into mud, which clumped on their shoes making each step a real effort.

They were half a mile from the car when Bret stopped and stood squinting through the trees. Then he pointed. "Look!"

She gazed in the direction he indicated but at first couldn't see anything. The clouds overhead shifted for just a second, letting a shaft of moonlight shine through. Ginny glimpsed the most beautiful thing she'd ever seen—the roof of a cabin.

She breathed a prayer of thanks as Bret grabbed her hand and pulled her toward it. He was like a horse that had spotted its own barn door and was anxious to get to its feed bag.

Slipping and sliding in the mud, she followed as he used his flashlight to illuminate the way.

"How did you spot this?" she asked, struggling to keep up.

"Saw the gap in the trees."

Ginny grimaced at his back. He didn't have to sound so insufferably smug. If she hadn't been walking with her head down, feeling sorry for herself, she might have been the one to notice the place.

They reached the cabin, a tiny affair built over an open carport. Shaky stairs led up to the front door. They ran up them carefully and began pounding on the door simultaneously. They paused to wait for a response and when no answer came pounded again.

The rain increased steadily as they stood there. Any last dry spots on either of them were now soaked. Finally Bret turned to her, wiped water from his eyes and stated the obvious. "There's no one home."

"N-no k-kidding," she stammered.

"We've only got one choice."

"What?"

"We're going to break in."

# CHAPTER SEVEN

"I THOUGHT YOU SAID you weren't a lock picker."
Ginny punctuated her statement with a sneeze, then
rubbed her cold-numbed face.

"I'm not going to pick it. I'm going to break in."

Horrified, Ginny stared at him. "Oh, no! Can't we
just wait in the carport until the storm blows over? I'll
bet it's dry in there."

Bret looked at her, undoubtedly seeing her weari-
ness. She was shivering uncontrollably now, her slen-
der body shuddering so hard it rattled a loose wooden
panel on the floor of the landing. "You'll have double pneumonia by then. Don't worry. I'll pay the
owner for any damages." He leaned closer to inspect
the lock, then grunted in surprise. "There probably
won't be any damage—I can open this thing with a
credit card."

While Ginny watched, he slid a card from his wal-
let, inserted it between the doorjamb and the lock—
and promptly snapped the plastic card into two neat
halves.

Despite her suffering, Ginny laughed at the stunned
expression on his face. "Did you learn that from your
friends on the vice squad?"

"The darn thing must be frozen." Utterly disgusted, he stuffed the pieces back into his pocket.

"Let's face it," she said, nudging him aside. "This isn't your area of expertise."

"Oh, and I suppose it's yours."

"We'll never know until I try. If we're going to do this, let's do it right." She searched in her soggy bag for a moment and came up with a nail file. "Hold the light steady," she ordered.

Bret might have argued if he hadn't been as cold and miserable as she was. Ginny had a little trouble getting her icy fingers to cooperate but finally managed to ease the file into just the right position and spring the lock. The door opened, allowing musty air to rush out.

"My hero," Bret muttered, hustling her inside. He shone the flashlight around the tiny cabin's one room, found a light switch and flipped it on, but nothing happened. "The electricity must be turned off for the winter," he said, then looked to see what else the cabin had to offer.

The furniture was sparse and simple: a sagging sofa, a few rickety chairs around a spindly coffee table and two bare bunk beds built into a wall; there was a tiny kitchen area in one corner. But they barely noticed these things as they searched for a more important item. They both sighed with relief when they found what they were looking for—a wood-burning stove. They were also pleased that beside it was an old-fashioned coal scuttle containing twists of paper and chunks of kindling.

Within minutes, Bret had laid the beginnings of a fire, rushed down to the carport for some stove-length logs he'd noticed there and had a fire blazing with the aid of matches he'd discovered in the scuttle. Blessed warmth soon began radiating into the small room.

Somehow, feeling the warmth made Ginny even colder. She shook harder than ever, great racking tremors that started from deep within her. It was as if opening the cabin door had used up the last of her strength, and she could no longer control her muscles.

"You've got to get out of those wet things," Bret insisted, glancing around. He found a kerosene lamp and lit it, then spied a closet. He swung the open door and rummaged through it until he found a couple of old sweat suits. He tossed one to her and kept the other for himself.

"Th-thank you," Ginny said, failing to stop her teeth from chattering. "W-where's the bathroom?"

He snorted with laughter as he stripped off his jacket, then his shirt. The glow from the lamp bathed his smooth hair-dusted chest with golden light. "Honey, this is a cabin, not a five-star hotel. You'll have to change in here. I've seen you naked before, remember?" His voice was as smooth and bland as oatmeal, but there was a glint in his eyes that reminded her of chili peppers.

Ginny pressed her full lips together and tried to appear stern. The fact that he had seen her naked before was the *last* thing she wanted to remember at that moment. She was weak enough already and felt about as attractive as a wet skunk. With a grimace that said she wasn't happy but would tough this out, she grabbed the gray sweat suit and put her back to him. Bret made an appropriately derisive sound at her. A few seconds later, though, she heard the rustle of his clothing.

At lightning speed, she whisked off her jacket and shirt and pulled the oversize top over her head. She was grateful to see that it fell to midthigh. Knowing she was so well covered made her confident enough to ease off her muddy shoes, unzip her jeans and slide them down her legs. It took a bit of work to get the wet narrow-legged denim off, but she finally succeeded. Then she tugged on the sweatpants.

They were enormous. She had to pull the waist up almost to her armpits and roll up the hems to keep from tripping. Satisfied at last, she turned to spread her wet clothing about the room—and stopped short.

Bret hadn't finished changing his clothes. He had removed his jeans and was wearing sweatpants that matched hers. On him, they were snug, but the waist was stretched out so they rode low on his hips. He'd moved closer to the lamp, and since his chest was still bare she had an even better view of the familiar sandy-brown hair that swirled across his flat stomach. Slowly he shook out the shirt, then held it up to distinguish the front from the back, then eased it over his head.

Ginny tried to stop staring and swallow the lump that had formed in her throat, but didn't succeed until he'd pulled the shirt down. He combed his hands carelessly through his damp hair, smoothing it back from his face, then glanced up. "Something wrong?"

"N-no," she breathed, quickly grabbing two of the dilapidated wooden chairs close to the stove and spreading her clothes on one. He did the same, then went outside for more wood.

While he was gone, she went over to inspect the bunks, fully expecting them to be nothing more than mouse condos. She didn't relish the idea of spending the night there, because nothing in the little cabin was even close to clean. However, the bunks seemed fairly solid, although the slats were a bit loose. Piles of dust that matched ones she'd seen underneath the windows made her wonder if the place was infested with termites, but she decided the bunks would be okay, as long as they were careful.

Cautiously she unrolled the mattresses that sat on the ends of the beds and was relieved to see they held nothing more ominous than dirt and a few dead bugs, which she whisked to the floor. She was happy to know she and Bret would each have their own bed tonight. Now all she had to do was scrounge up pillows and blankets.

"It's stopped raining," Bret announced as he reentered with a final load of wood. He dumped it beside the stove. "We should be able to get to the highway for help in the morning." He shook his head when he saw she was about to speak. "Don't say it, Ginny. We're not going back out there tonight even if the rain *does* stop. We're both still chilled to the bone."

Actually she wasn't anymore. Seeing his bare chest and knowing they were going to spend the night together for the first time in eight months had warmed her. Nonetheless, she held her hands out to the heat emanating from the stove and nodded. "All right, Bret." She glanced at him. "I don't suppose there's any food?"

"I don't know. If there was any justice in this world, there'd be a seven-course dinner in that purse of yours."

Ginny stuck out her tongue at him. Chuckling, Bret moved to the tiny kitchen and looked through the cupboards. "Not a thing except some herb tea." He made a gagging sound, but held up the box and shook it invitingly. "It's probably stale, but I'm willing to try it if you are."

He seemed so at ease with her she suddenly felt foolish. He obviously didn't see her the way she saw him. And why should he? She'd spent the past several weeks ensuring that he knew theirs was strictly a working relationship. It was only *her* knees that turned to water at the sight of his well-remembered body and the memory of his kisses. Ever since the county fair she'd had all kinds of crazy wishes and desires, none of which she would pursue. He'd indicated that *he* wanted to pursue them, but she wasn't going to take him up on his subtle offers, or his not-so-subtle ones, for that matter.

She wandered over to join him. "Great idea, but where do we get the water and how do we heat it? There's no running water in here."

Bret's crooked smile mocked her. "Have a little faith in me, will you?" He grabbed the teakettle and the flashlight and headed for the door. "I saw a hand pump outside. And the top of that stove is flat for a reason, you know. We can set the kettle on that."

They did as he suggested and in a short time had steaming cups of a surprisingly tasty brew to sip. Bret dragged the couch cushions and some pillows over to the stove and made a warm nest for them on a faded rag rug.

Ginny eyed it suspiciously for a moment, but Bret seemed so genuinely pleased with his arrangement and it looked so inviting that she joined him there, settling back against a cushion and balancing her cup on the thick layers of fleece covering her stomach. A few sips of the tea soothed her and she began to relax.

If anyone had asked she couldn't have named all the emotions she was feeling—wary, yet happy to be alone with Bret, as well as oddly piqued that he was treating her the way he'd treat one of his sisters.

Bret took a swallow of his own tea, grimaced and said, "Are you comfortable?"

"Yes."

"Warm enough?"

"Yes."

They both fell silent, the crackle of the fire the only sound in the cabin. Ginny's gaze fell on his long legs stretched out toward the blaze visible through the glass fire doors. His bare toes twitched and he rubbed the top of one foot over the other. She remembered the movement as something he did when deep in thought.

Suddenly memories of the two of them alone together came flooding back. She had worked ruthlessly to keep them buried, but now she seemed to be at their mercy, unable to stop them from bombarding her.

"We're alone together, Ginny," he said, startling her into thinking he could read her mind.

She shot him a quick nervous glance, then stared at the pale liquid in her cup. "I know."

"We'll be here all night. I'm wondering if you knew that when you locked the keys in the car."

She sat up straight. "What?"

"Some kind of subconscious slip, maybe?" He set his cup down and leaned back on the cushions, his posture easy and relaxed.

"Bret, have you lost your mind?"

He gave an uncaring shrug, but in the pale light, she could see the sharp alertness in his eyes. "No. I'm just wondering if it's possible you realized it's time for us to have a talk."

She moved ever so slightly away from him. "About what?"

"About why you left me. It's been more than a month since I last asked you. Like I said I'm a patient man, but I deserve to know the truth."

Dismayed, she stared at him. She'd hoped he'd decided to drop the subject. Of course she'd hoped in vain—stubbornness was too much a part of him.

Absently she put down her cup and started to rise. He grabbed her wrist and pulled her back so hard she fell across his lap. With a soft sound of alarm, she scrambled off him.

"Running away? Where are you planning to go, honey?" His voice was gentle, as if soothing a skittish foal, but in his eyes intense purpose burned. "It's wet and cold outside, and besides, I've hidden your shoes."

"You did *what?*" she squeaked, glancing around for them.

"I hid them when I went out for more wood." He released his hold on her wrist. "So you might as well stay and deal with this."

She understood now that he'd been biding his time. All these weeks when she'd thought he was willing to forget the past, he'd merely been waiting for the right moment. Obviously, in his mind, it had come.

"Unless you really are the coward I accused you of being," he taunted.

That awoke her pride, as he had probably known it would. "I'm not afraid."

"So tell me."

The simple demand shook her far more than badgering would have. She was well aware of how relentless he could be when interviewing someone he thought was lying. Grateful to be spared that, she took a deep breath and began, deciding that she had to try to tell him.

"After the first month I felt as if I'd married a stranger. The timing was wrong. We'd married too soon after we'd met."

"When something's right, you don't need to waste time waiting. Our marriage was right."

"Not for me." She picked up her cup, more for something to occupy her hands than to quench her thirst. "*I* needed more time. I needed to know my family approved." She sent him a pleading glance. "My father and I had a terrible argument the night before you and I went down to city hall and got married."

Bret sat forward, studying her. "He likes me now. He wouldn't have hired me if he didn't."

"Yes, and I'm . . . I'm glad, but . . ."

"But you can't leave the past behind?"

Ginny placed her cup on the floor, then ran her hands through her hair in frustration. "It's not just that. I thought everything would be all right once we were actually husband and wife." She licked her lips nervously and saw his gaze shift to the betraying gesture. This was harder than she'd thought. Words had always come easily to her, but now the ones she wanted seemed to be buried too deeply. "After we moved in together, I never saw you. It wasn't like I thought marriage should be."

"What did you think it should be?"

She shrugged and the wide neck of her sweatshirt slipped down her shoulder. Impatiently she tugged it back into place. "Like the one my parents had." She started nibbling at one of her nails, but he pulled her hand away. Bothered by his touch, she twisted her wrist from his grasp. Her troubled eyes met his, which were steady and direct as if trying to see into her thoughts.

"Don't you think you could have been romanticizing things? Your mother died when you were twelve." When anger flared in her eyes he held up his hands. "Wait a minute. Let me finish. I lost my dad when I was about the same age, remember? I know what it was like." He stopped and blew out a breath. "I'm not saying what you thought about your parents' marriage was wrong, but maybe you had a child's view of what marriage was like and didn't give us time to work things out."

Ginny dropped her head into her hands and rubbed her temples. "Bret, how could we work things out if you were never home? I hardly ever saw you."

"I'm here now."

His quiet statement brought her head up. Her blue eyes were clouded with worry, and she crossed her arms over her chest in an unconsciously protective gesture. "But for how long?"

"I've already told you I'm here to stay. We can work out all our problems."

"There's no need for that, Bret. We're divorced."

"Funny, I don't feel divorced. Especially not at this moment."

He moved closer, mesmerizing her with his gentleness. He unfolded her arms as easily as if they were strips of paper and slid his hands along her sides and over her back, drawing her to him.

"Oh, Bret, please don't." Her pounding heart was interfering with her breathing, making her voice reedy.

"Don't what?" he asked, holding her eyes with his own. "Don't want you? Sorry, can't do it. Don't hold you? Can't do that, either. Don't kiss you? You're asking the impossible. I've thought of nothing else since that night at the county fair." He didn't give her time to protest further, but eased her back against the pillows and settled his lips on hers.

She knew she should have resisted—any woman worth her salt would have—but she couldn't. With a soft murmur of assent, she allowed herself to take a dizzying ride back in time. This was what she remembered. His lips warm and firm, possessive and wonderful, his hands cradling her face in a way that never failed to turn her insides to the consistency of warm honey. Once again he was making her feel as if she was the most precious thing he'd ever held. How could she resist him?

Ginny didn't even try. She kissed him and reveled in the feeling of rightness that flooded through her. Eager to touch him, she let her hands wander over his shoulders and down the sinewy length of his arms, reacquainting herself with his strength, recalling how beautiful and satisfying things had once been between them.

With no hesitation, caution or concern, she met his needs and offered her own for him to satisfy. No one else had ever treated her this way, as if he would die if he couldn't touch her, feel her touching him. For long moments she was everything to him and he to her.

"You've lost weight," he whispered against the warm skin of her throat, and she realized his hands were under her baggy sweatshirt, spanning her rib cage, his fingers almost meeting at her spine. "What have you been doing to yourself?"

She was too overcome by emotions to worry about protecting any secrets she might have. "I couldn't eat much when I came home. I was worried about Dad and about leaving you. I felt like such a . . ." Barely in time, sanity returned, and she stopped herself before she said too much.

Bret jerked as if she'd pinched him and pulled away slightly. The passion in his eyes was joined by a dawning understanding. He cupped her jaw so she couldn't look away. "What? What were you about to say?"

She gasped as if she'd just been hit with a faceful of cold water. "N-nothing," she stammered, desperately trying to gather her thoughts. She wrenched her chin from his firm grasp and shifted away from him, her hands busily pulling down her shirt and smoothing her hair. Bret let her go, but as she jumped to her feet, she could feel his intensity all but dragging her back.

He wasn't about to let her escape. He followed her as she stood. She was stunned by what she'd almost said, and she prayed he wouldn't pursue the topic.

They stood face-to-face before the sturdy little stove. The heat it gave off was nothing compared to what she had just felt in Bret's arms. What had she been thinking? If she let herself fall in love with him again she'd be worse off than ever if he left. That's what she feared—loving him again and then failing to keep him interested. And then she'd be alone once more. Frightened and confused, she twisted her hands in the hem of her fleecy shirt.

"Ginny," he coaxed, "tell me what you were going to say."

She shook her head so that her pale hair belled around her narrow chin. "It's not important. It doesn't matter now."

"Yes, it does." He took a step closer and she nervously danced aside. "You were about to finally tell me how you really felt about leaving me."

"I've said as much as I want to." She moved away, hitching up her baggy pants with one hand and picking up pillows and tossing them onto the bunks with the other. Then she grabbed the lamp and went to the closet where she searched for blankets. She found two moth-eaten ones that would do if they kept a good fire going in the stove. Shaking them out, she wrinkled her nose at the musty smell. She glanced up to see Bret watching her.

He came toward her, lifting his hand and pointing a finger at her. "You're not going to get away with this forever, you know. Someday, somehow, you're going to tell me everything."

She threw a blanket at him, and he caught it easily. "I don't have anything else to say."

He made a sound of disgust and anger flared in his gray eyes. "You're afraid. Why don't you just admit it?"

Righteously indignant, she splayed a hand over her chest and bent slightly from the waist. "Afraid? Of what?"

"Of your own feelings! Good Lord, you're going to be twenty-four next month. Isn't it time you grew up and faced things?"

"Face things?" she was almost shouting, her anger fueled by frustrated desire, irritation and the fear she wouldn't admit to him. "I face things just fine, thank you. Maybe you should face the fact that I want you to keep your hands to yourself from now on."

Bret's eyes widened. "Don't add lying to your crimes!" In an angry gesture he pointed to the place on the floor where moments before they'd been kissing. "Not five minutes ago you wanted me as much as I wanted you!"

Because she couldn't deny it and was too embarrassed to admit it, she gave him a forbidding look and changed the subject. "Which bunk do you want?"

Bret looked as if he was ready to strangle her. "You're the most frustrating woman I've ever met, do you know that?"

"Which bunk do you want?"

He threw his hands in the air. "I don't care! Heaven forbid we should share one!"

"Okay. I'll take the top one."

"Okay. I'll let you." He stopped and drew a breath. "How are you going to get up there? There's no ladder."

"I'll jump," she said, stalking over to toss her blanket on the grungy mattress and fluff the ancient pillows.

"I'll get you a chair."

"No, thank you." Her face was as stiff as her voice as she glanced at him. Their eyes met.

"You're being unreasonable."

Her eyes skittered away. She knew she was, but she couldn't help it. Emotions she hadn't allowed herself to feel in months were overwhelming her. The defenses she had so carefully built to keep herself from loving him again were collapsing faster than a sand castle at high tide.

With a defeated slump of his shoulders, Bret added more wood to the fire and closed the glass doors. He took the kerosene lantern from her and moved toward the lower bunk. "I'll turn this off when you're safely in bed."

"All right." She backed up, gauging the distance to the top bunk.

"Are you sure you want to do this?" he asked uncertainly, sitting on his bunk, then lying down. He plumped his pillow, put his hands under his head and turned to watch her.

"Of course. This'll be easy. I was a gymnast in high school, remember? This can't be any harder than vaulting. All I need is a running start." She hitched up her pants once again, then rolled up the cuffs, making sure she wouldn't trip as she made the leap.

"Why don't you let me give you a hand up?"

"No! I can do this."

"Well, then, do it!"

Her eyes flashing with irritation, she stepped back a few more paces. Then, swinging her arms forward lightly, she lifted herself onto her toes and dashed toward the bunk. She jumped, slapped her hands onto the outside rail and twisted in midair so that she'd come down on her bottom. When she landed she felt a moment of elation . . . just before the rotten boards broke and she fell through.

# CHAPTER EIGHT

"YEOW!" BRET SQUAWKED as the boards, mattress—and Ginny—crashed down on top of him. When their combined weights hit, the boards on his bunk gave way, too, and then everything fell to the wooden floor.

Ginny lay stunned, blinking at the ceiling and trying to catch the breath that had been knocked out of her. It was several seconds before a groaning sound registered in her brain, and she realized she wasn't the one making it.

"Bret," she gasped, rolling off what was left of her bunk and onto her knees. Frantically she tugged the mattress out of the way. "Bret, are you all right? Oh, please, tell me you're all right!"

Once the mattress was removed, she saw that he was trapped in a prison of broken boards. He looked as stunned as she felt, but she couldn't see any visible injuries. On her hands and knees, she scrambled forward for a better look. He didn't seem to be bleeding. Of course, he still could have sustained internal injuries.

Bret stared up at her and shook his head slowly from side to side. His lips moved, but no words came out.

Ginny began tearing out boards and tossing them behind her. She cleared a path to him, all the while babbling in a high frantic voice. "I'm so sorry. I didn't know this would happen...I didn't even think... The bunks seemed sturdy enough... Are you all right? Are you hurt? Why aren't you talking?''

"Talk?" he finally wheezed, cradling his stomach and chest. "I can hardly breathe!''

"Oh, no. I've really hurt you, haven't I?" Her head whipped around as she futilely searched the cabin for some form of help. "There's no phone here. Why didn't the stupid owner put in a phone?''

"Maybe he wasn't expecting anyone to force their way in and use the bunk for a trampoline,'' Bret suggested mildly, trying to sit up at last.

Ginny barely heard him. "I can't call an ambulance. Oh, why did I lock the keys in the car? How idiotic can one person be?''

Bret groaned and touched her hand. "Why don't you put your panic on hold, honey? Instead, could you help me get out of here?''

"Oh, of course." She reached into what was left of the bunks. A few boards were still partially attached to the top bunk, their jagged broken ends hanging just above Ginny's head. She pushed them out of the way to clear a path for Bret. When he had moved close enough to the side, she put her hands under his arms to lend him her strength.

With her steadying him, Bret managed to get his balance and crawl slowly out of the wreckage. "Let's be grateful the floor is holding,'' he grumbled as he climbed stiffly over the side and sat down near her to catch his breath. "Otherwise we'd be spending the night in the carport.''

"It was the termites,'' Ginny told him. "I knew those boards didn't look safe.''

He gave her a level stare. "Then why did you insist on jumping up there?"

"I forgot," she answered in a small contrite voice, her blue eyes filled with dismay. She laid a tentative hand on his arm. "Are...are you all right? Let me see your back." She got on her knees beside him. He turned around carefully. She eased his sweatshirt up to check for injuries. Other than a few red streaks where the boards had hit his right side when he'd lifted his arm to protect his head, he appeared fine. Unable to stop herself, she leaned forward and kissed the reddest spot just above the loose waistband of his sweatpants.

Bret trembled and sucked in his breath. "Ginny..."

"Oh! I'm sorry, Bret. I...I don't know what I was..." With nerveless fingers, she smoothed his shirt into place.

"Never mind. I've got a number of sorer places I'd like you to kiss, but I don't think you're ready for that." He regarded her over his shoulder.

"I'm not?" she asked, looking everywhere but at him. Of course she wasn't. She wasn't ready to be this close to him. She didn't know what to feel. Only moments ago she'd been righteously indignant, then foolishly careless, and look what had happened.

"No, you're not. Let's just say it's too bad we didn't have kids. I'm wondering if I'll ever be a father."

It took a few seconds for his meaning to register. When it did Ginny's face reddened.

With a faint grin he glanced away from her and pointed to the kerosene lamp. "I'm glad that thing didn't break. We'd be fighting a fire right now." He cocked an eyebrow at her. "Maybe I should join the Webster volunteer fire department. If I keep hanging around with you I might need to know a few lifesaving techniques."

Insulted, she glared at him. "I know this fiasco is my fault. You don't have to keep rubbing it in."

He relented and shrugged. The motion made him wince and she felt sorry for her thoughtless actions all over again. "Let's put the mattresses over by the stove. That's what we should have done in the first place."

"I'll do it." Ginny jumped to her feet and dragged the mattresses across the floor. She positioned them on the rag rug, several inches apart, then hurried back for the two thin blankets and the pillows.

Shakily Bret got to his feet and followed her. He looked at the arrangement she had made and said dryly, "There's no way I'm letting you get even that far away from me. I'm afraid you'll get up in the middle of the night to put wood in the stove and set my hair on fire."

She clapped her hands onto her hips. "Now wait a minute, mister—"

"Save it, Ginny," he muttered as he lowered himself gingerly to his knees and pulled one mattress on top of the other. "We'll sleep together. It's wide enough and we'll be more comfortable that way, not to mention warmer."

She knew he was in no mood to argue, but she hoped to stall the inevitable a little longer. "Wouldn't you like me to make a cold compress for your ribs, or, uh..?"

"No, Ginny, I don't. Let's just get some sleep." He lay down and waited while she arranged the blankets. When she hesitated to join him he flipped back the edges of the blankets and said, "It's not as if it's the first time we've ever slept together, Ginny, but believe me, this won't be like any of those other times.''

Oh, yes, it would. Simply being close to him was difficult. Sleeping with him, even platonically, would be awful. Or would it? She recalled the eight months' worth of dreams from which she'd awakened and moved her hand over to the other pillow to see if he was there. At least this way she knew where he was. She looked into his eyes and couldn't hide the longing in her own.

He sat up halfway. ''Ginny...''

''All right,'' she said, kneeling on the mattresses. ''I ... I guess it'll be okay.''

He hesitated for a second and she froze in anticipation, but he simply turned onto his side and waited for her to lie down beside him, then moved her so that her bottom was nestled against his thighs and his arm was around her waist.

Ginny settled her head in the crook of his arm. She knew this wasn't a good idea, but for once she was going to ignore her doubts and fears. Something brushed her hair and she wondered if it was his lips. She snuggled closer and consciously relaxed her muscles. There was no denying she felt safe for the first time in months. Safe and cared for.

Bret stirred and turned out the lamp, then placed his arm around her once more. The glow from the glass doors on the wood-burning stove gave the room faint illumination. Satisfied, Ginny let her eyes flutter shut. She was almost asleep when Bret spoke again.

''You're right about one thing, Ginny.''

''What's that?'' she murmured, too secure and content to wake up completely.

"We got married too quickly. We needed to get to know each other. We can't go back in time, but we can start over."

She was awake now. She turned her head, trying to read his face in the dimness. "We can?"

"Yes, and that's exactly what we're going to do. We're going to start dating."

"DATING?" Carrie's voice hooted over the phone line. "I thought you were trying to keep your distance from him. At least that's what you said the last time I was home."

"Well, things have changed. Besides, this is his idea. I didn't say I'd go along with it." Ginny ran a brush through her hair as she talked to her sister. She had showered and dried her hair, then dressed in a pair of black stirrup pants and a flowing white top. Feeling restless and curiously let down after the strange and exciting night she'd just spent, she had called her sister. She told herself it was to report on their father's well-being, but she also needed to hear a familiar voice.

That morning, it had taken Ginny and Bret an hour to walk to a phone and get a locksmith and tow truck out to help them. Once they had unlocked the car and the radiator hose was repaired, though, it hadn't taken them long to reach home. Fortunately the owner of Hugh's cabin knew the owner of the cabin where Ginny and Bret had been stranded. They were able to get his phone number, explain about the damage and offer to pay for it. The man was considering the matter. They just hoped he wouldn't decide to press charges against them. But Ginny wasn't really worried about that; she was still trying to sort out her feelings for Bret.

"You don't sound as if you'll fight him very hard," Carrie observed. "Exactly what is it you want?"

"I want to be sure I'm making the right decision this time." That was the only thing of which she was certain.

"Remember last fall when I started talking about college?"

"Of course."

"You told me the best way to find the one that was right for me was to get as much information as possible about all the ones I was considering."

Ginny wound the phone cord around her fingers. "So, what's your point?"

Carrie made an exasperated noise. "So, find out as much as you can about Bret this time. If he's not right for you, you'll know. Jeez, Ginny, do I have to tell you everything?"

Laughing, Ginny finished the conversation and hung up. It *was* time for her to take her own advice. She simply needed to think the situation through carefully and decide what was best.

Ginny sat down on her bed, then jumped up again and paced to the window. Glancing outside, she saw that the sun had come out and dried up some of the night's rain. She could start raking the leaves that had blown down in the storm. Hugh had hired Jimmy Blaines to do the job, but Ginny knew if she didn't do something physical, she'd go crazy. Besides, clouds were building up as if they were preparing to drench the countryside once more. If she wanted to get the job done, she needed to do it now.

She threw a jacket on and hurried outside to find the rake and some trash bags. As she worked she thought about all that had happened in the past few weeks. She'd been furious when Hugh had taken her job away from her, but she had to admit it had turned out well. Bret was doing a wonderful job, and she was happy just reporting the news.

Another of her worries had been that winning the MacKellar Award would quicken Bret's disenchantment with a small-town newspaper, but he showed no signs of that. If anything he was coming up with even more ideas for improving the *Herald*. He had joined a number of civic organizations, as well, and was making himself generally indispensable.

At first she'd wondered if she had been flattering herself when she thought Bret had moved to Webster in an attempt to get her back. What man would want the woman who had left him, injured and hospitalized, to run back to her father? He certainly hadn't been shy about showing his contempt for her cowardice. But now she wasn't sure what to think.

Then there was her concern that Bret would get too close to her again, that he would become too important. She realized that's exactly what *had* happened, though in a different way. He was now giving her something she'd longed for during their marriage— respect and courtesy. At the office he listened to her ideas and gave her full credit if he used them. When they talked she had his full attention. When they kissed, well, she would just about follow him anywhere for one of those kisses. . . .

Deep in thought, Ginny didn't hear the footsteps behind her. When Bret spoke she gasped and whirled around. He, too, had showered and changed, and was now in clean corduroy slacks and a sweater in shades of gold and warm brown. He also wore a leather bomber jacket, which made him look appealing yet dangerous.

"Good afternoon, miss."

"Miss?" She laughed at the word, then sobered at the odd expression on his face. It was as if his eyes were seeing a stranger; there was no recognition in them. A thrill of apprehension raced up her spine.

"How do you do? I'm Bret Calhoun. I couldn't help noticing you out here slaving away." He took the rake from her suddenly lax fingers. "Would you like some help?"

She blinked. "Bret, did that bunk hit you in the head last night?"

He frowned. "Hey, I've got this all planned. Don't spoil it. We're supposed to start again, right?"

"Right." She stretched the word out cautiously.

"I don't know of any better way to start than with an introduction." He assumed his stranger's pose again and said, "And your name is...?"

"This is ridiculous."

"Humor me." With a long-suffering look on his face, he touched his right side. "I'm an injured man. Now, what was your name?"

Instantly contrite because she was the one who had caused his injury, she answered. "Ginny McCoy."

His eyes lit up. "Ah, the real McCoy. I've found you at last."

Ginny's lips trembled as she recalled the day they'd met at Sam and Laura's wedding. He had said the very same words to her then, and look where they'd taken her! "Oh, Bret, I don't know if this is such a good idea."

"Do you have a better one?"

"Well, no."

"Is starting over the right thing to do?"

"That depends on where it will lead. Where *will* it lead?"

He widened his eyes and lifted his eyebrows until he was the picture of innocence. "Wherever you want it to lead."

Ginny pressed her hands together over her stomach and turned away from him. When she turned back, her eyes were troubled. "I want to know the truth, Bret. Why did you move to Webster? And do you really plan to stay? With the MacKellar Award you could write your own ticket at any paper in the South—or in the country, for that matter."

Bret paused before answering her and looked out across the lawn, which was dappled with pale sunlight and strewn with leaves. A gust of wind ruffled his hair and he smoothed it down with an absent gesture. When he finally spoke his voice was distant. "Did I ever tell you why I became a newspaperman, Ginny?"

"No, never."

He gave her a rueful glance as if he was laughing at himself. "I saw it as one of the last opportunities for an honest man to make a difference in the world."

"And you don't feel that way now?"

"I guess I began to realize that wasn't the case. Reporting wasn't all altruism and the right to know. It was about competition and ego, too. I became so competitive over my stories, my contacts, my sources, that sometimes I reminded myself of a dog fighting over a bone."

Ginny grimaced at the description. She had never thought of him like that, though she'd known he was very determined.

"Not a pretty picture, is it? I became so hard-nosed and driven that I lost the most important thing in my life."

The directness of his gaze told her that the important thing had been her. But she was relieved when he didn't say it. Hearing it put into words would place pressure on her for which she wasn't prepared. Right now she'd be satisfied with what he'd said, and let the answers to her questions come in time. After all, she hadn't told him everything he wanted to know.

Since he'd come to town, she'd been trying to get all the answers at once so that the future could be settled and secure. The experiences of her adolescence—her mother's death, Hugh's short bout with a drinking problem, helping to raise Carrie and putting off her own plans for college and a career—should have told her that life wasn't always settled and secure.

But she'd wanted a guarantee that things would work out fine, that Bret would always be there. That she'd never be alone. Maybe she should just relax and let things happen, because no one could control the future.

Reading the war of emotions on her face, Bret offered her a sympathetic smile, then moved near to place an arm around her shoulder. It made her think of the way they had slept on the hard floor of the rickety cabin the night before. It was comforting, yet not demanding. "How about it? Need some help?"

"Sure." When she smiled up at him, she noticed the darkening sky. "But we'd better hurry. It's going to rain again."

He nodded and took the rake. She held the trash bag open as he scooped up leaves and deposited them inside. When they finished Bret invited her to dinner. She accepted happily and they went to a little café that had the best barbecue in the county. They ate too much of the sticky crisp ribs and helped each other clean up the sauce that had dribbled down their chins. Groaning, they headed home, each blaming the other for their overindulgence. On the way, they rented a movie and when they got home watched it, curled up together on the couch in the den. By the time he left, she was exhausted. She fell into bed, too tired to miss her father.

That set the pattern for the entire week. Ginny and Bret worked agreeably together. At the paper she didn't always agree with him and often fought him on decisions, but she still respected him.

Bret's bruised ribs healed, and the owner of the cabin called to say he was going to have the place torn down. He'd decided that it was a hazard. Ginny floated along in a blissful daze, for once unconcerned about Bret's motives or possible departure. She was determined to accept things as they came.

In the evenings work was left behind. Bret concentrated solely on her. It was exhilarating and flattering, but also scary to have his full attention in a way she hadn't since the early days of their marriage.

He teased her about her nail-biting and suggested she have a manicure, reasoning that if she paid for her nail care, she'd be less inclined to bite them. He reminded her that with a name like McCoy there was the soul of a parsimonious old Scot lurking inside her somewhere; she wouldn't ruin something she'd paid for. Although she didn't much care for his brand of reasoning, she tried it and it worked. Proudly she showed her fingers to Doris, who opened her little metal box and gave back all the money she'd collected over the past months. Ginny used the money to take Bret to dinner.

On Friday Bret asked her to come with him to Sam and Laura's. He'd been invited to dinner on the condition he'd help Sam put up the last of the wallpaper in the baby's room. Ginny eagerly accepted.

The rain that had battered Webster off and on for a week was threatening again, and the temperature had dropped, promising icy streets. Dark clouds covered the sky as they turned into the driveway of Sam and Laura's big Victorian house.

"I've always loved this place," Ginny said with a sigh, looking at the glow of lamps that sent their welcoming light into the falling dusk. "When I was a little girl my mother dressed me up in my Sunday best, right down to my black patent-leather shoes, and brought me to tea with Miss McCord, Laura's great-aunt. She told me all about the tea parties she and Laura had during their visits. Funny, I knew about Laura years before I ever met her."

Bret chuckled softly as he stepped from the car and came around to open her door. "So did Sam. Miss McCord made sure he knew plenty about Laura, then fixed it so that he was executor of her estate and Laura inherited everything. Very cozy, the way she got them together."

"I don't think they mind," Ginny said, wondering whether things would have been different if she had known more about Bret before they'd married. She felt a moment of envy for Sam and Laura's settled life—the cats Laura had inherited along with the home, Sam's work training his beautiful pointers and most of all the child they were expecting. But then Laura opened the front door and stood smiling in welcome, a couple of big fluffy felines wrapping themselves around her ankles, and Ginny could feel nothing but joy for her friend.

If Sam and Laura were surprised that Ginny had arrived with Bret, they hid it well. They seemed delighted to see her. While Sam and Bret went to find the wallpapering tools, Laura invited Ginny upstairs to see the baby's room. As they went, Laura told Ginny about the changes and improvements they'd made to the house in the past couple of years.

Before their marriage Sam had lived next door, where he had kennels for his dogs in the yard. After they'd married, Sam had turned his house into an office and moved his things into Laura's home. The dogs stayed in their kennels, and the cats reigned supreme in the sun room he'd built for them off the kitchen.

Laura stopped halfway up the staircase to catch her breath. Seeing Ginny's alarm, she smiled. "I've just been talking too much. If this baby doesn't come soon, I'm staying downstairs for the duration. Thank goodness Sam put a bathroom in near the kitchen."

"Are you sure you should be climbing these?" Ginny asked, following as Laura resumed her laborious ascent.

"Goo... good exercise," Laura panted.

Ginny's concern was momentarily forgotten as the two of them walked into the bright airy nursery. "This is lovely," she said, unable to keep the envy from her voice. The room had been painted a soft peach and decorated in a carousel theme. A roll of the wallpaper Laura had chosen was spread on top of the changing table. It was a whimsical pattern of carousel animals in pastel shades.

Laura ran her hand over a baby quilt that had been placed in the spooled maple crib. "I think we've gone a little crazy," she confessed, "but it is our first child."

Ginny walked over and gave her a hug. "You're entitled." She ducked her head so her unexpected tears wouldn't be quite as noticeable, then turned gladly when she heard the men coming.

"I thought we were all finished decorating," Sam groused. His arms were loaded with tubs of wallpaper paste, smoothing brushes and rollers. "We've re-done this house from top to bottom."

"Oh, don't complain," Laura said, standing on tiptoe to place a light kiss on his jaw. "I saw this wallpaper and I knew it was just the thing for the baby's room. You want your child to have nothing but the best, don't you? And it's only one wall." She batted her eyelashes at him in playful persuasion.

Sam chuckled. "Give an inch and she takes a mile. Come on, Bret, let's get busy. It's going to rain again, and I don't want this project ruined by too much moisture." He gave his wife a quick kiss and set to work.

Bret hesitated. Ginny could feel his eyes on her as she longingly examined the picture-perfect little room once more. The corner of his mouth tilted up as if he understood exactly what she was thinking. Warmth and closeness flowed between them as if she had just stepped into his embrace.

Oblivious to the undercurrents between Bret and Ginny, Laura turned to her with pleasure lighting her pretty face. "Let's go back downstairs and finish making dinner. I know from experience that these two men'll be starved when they're done.''

Ginny followed, thinking of how much happier she was when she didn't try to figure out everything that was happening between her and Bret.

In the kitchen, Laura stirred a pot of fragrant soup while her guest set the table. Ginny looked up in time to see Laura stretch onto her toes and reach into a cabinet for a bowl. She winced and leaned against the countertop, placing her forehead on the cupboard door.

Ginny rushed forward. "Are you all right?" she asked, helping Laura into a sturdy oak chair.

"Only a twinge," Laura insisted. "Nothing to worry about. I have these all the time."

"Why don't you sit and relax? I'll finish this." Ginny pulled another chair out and lifted Laura's feet onto it.

"Maybe I will. In two or three weeks I won't be able to pamper myself like this." She wiggled down in the chair and rested her head against the carved and polished back, then linked her fingers across her stomach.

Neither spoke as Ginny wrapped fresh bread in foil and placed it in the oven to heat, then sliced butter into neat even pats.

"How are things going between you and Bret?" Laura asked suddenly. When she saw Ginny's start of surprise, she laughed softly. "Did you think Sam and I weren't wondering?"

"I didn't know what you thought," Ginny admitted, turning the knife over and over in her hand.

"Sam says Bret is the stubbornest, most determined of all the Calhouns, and believe me, that's no recommendation in my book. I thought Sam was the stubbornest male I'd ever met, but maybe Bret is worse, just quieter about it. He wants you back, doesn't he?''

Ginny laid the butter knife precisely on the dish and set it on the table. "He seems to."

"And what do you want?"

The question, though asked softly, echoed through Ginny's mind like a dinner gong. Here, in this cozy kitchen, this happy home, she knew she couldn't avoid the truth. "To not get hurt again—or to hurt Bret."

"He was terribly hurt last winter. He came here one day and sat in the den with Sam for hours, talking about it."

Ginny looked down at her hands as they rested on the table. She felt like a murderer. When she didn't answer Laura continued, "You know, whatever happened can be fixed—if you want it to be."

Tears threatened and when Ginny spoke they clogged her throat. "That's a big 'if.'"

Laura said nothing for a moment, giving Ginny time to think things over, then she said in a more cheerful tone, "Do you know Bret proposed to me five minutes after meeting me?"

"No."

"He was only joking, of course. He just wanted to irritate Sam, but I wasn't surprised when you two married quickly. Bret has very definite ideas about what he wants."

And apparently Ginny was what he wanted, but since their adventures of the previous weekend and their talk the next day, she wasn't quite as worried about where things between them were leading. But she still didn't want to see either of them hurt.

When the bread was warmed and the soup ladled into a tureen, Ginny went upstairs to see if Bret and Sam were ready for dinner. They had just hung the last panel of wallpaper, and she complimented them on their work.

Sam washed up and headed downstairs, obviously eager to be with his wife. Standing at the top of the stairs, Bret rested his arm on Ginny's shoulders and drew her close for a slow kiss.

Surrendering to it, Ginny linked her hands behind him and savored the smooth firmness of his lips and the warmth of his embrace. His tenderness brought more tears to her eyes. She didn't realize they'd fallen until Bret nuzzled the moisture away. "What have you been thinking this evening?" he asked, gently rubbing his nose along her cheek.

She hesitated, but then lifted teary blue eyes to his. "I've been feeling jealous."

"Because of their baby?"

"Partly." Warmth flooded her cheeks. "But mostly because they seem so settled, so happy to be together."

"They went through some rough times when they first met, but they resolved their problems," Bret pointed out. "And they've been married more than a year now."

"Only two weeks longer than we would have been if..."

"If?"

When she didn't answer, he continued for her. "If you hadn't made the mistake of filing for divorce."

Feeling that their fragile truce was being threatened, she tilted her head back to glare at him, but he met her with a grin. He waggled his eyebrows suggestively and echoed what Laura had so recently said. "Mistakes can always be fixed, though. Maybe we can do a little fixing later tonight." He turned her and led her down the stairs once again. "I don't suppose you've had the urge to try some heavy-duty kissing in my new car yet, have you?"

She blushed and elbowed him. "Oh, stop it."

Their mood lightened, they joined the other couple for dinner. Ginny couldn't remember when she'd enjoyed herself so much—certainly not since she'd left Bret. That thought had her wondering if she really had been wrong to leave him.

They were just finishing dinner when the Webster fire whistle sounded. At the same time, Sam and Laura's phone began to ring. Neither of them answered it; Laura simply pushed herself to her feet and went to get Sam's jacket while he hurried into the den for his car keys. He was a volunteer fireman and would be needed, whatever the emergency.

Ginny saw Bret reaching for his own keys. She sat stiff with surprise as he rounded the table to give her an absentminded kiss. "I'm going along with Sam. I'll be back to pick you up later." He strode out of the room, calling to his sister-in-law, "Laura, do you have a camera I can borrow? I usually carry one in the car, but I left it at the office. I might be able to get a few shots for the paper."

Ginny rose slowly to her feet and stared after him. In a blinding flash she realized that nothing had changed. Bret was still willing to risk his life for a story. She tossed down the napkin she'd been holding and rushed after him.

Sam aimed a quick kiss at Laura's mouth and ran outside, holding his jacket over his head to shield himself from the rain that had begun pelting down.

Bret was checking over the camera Laura had handed him, his expert fingers familiarizing themselves with it. He was so engrossed that he jumped when Ginny clapped a hand onto his arm.

"Don't go," she insisted, fear entering her voice.

He looked at her in astonishment. "Don't go? Why not?"

"Because it's dangerous." *Because you might be hurt, or worse,* she added to herself.

"Sam's going." Puzzled, he turned to Laura for help, but she shrugged and walked away.

"Sam's a trained fireman," Ginny said. If Bret went now, she knew he didn't mean any of the things he had said. He might want her back, but he wouldn't change. He still needed the excitement that had driven his life in the city.

"I can take care of myself."

"Like you did during that drug bust?"

His jaw dropped. "Ginny, this is hardly the same thing."

"You don't know that!"

He slung the camera strap around his neck and tried to take her hands in his, but she backed away from him, feeling helpless and silly and scared.

He studied her panicked expression. "Can we talk about this when I get back?"

Defeated, with tears threatening, Ginny blinked to keep them from falling. "I won't be here when you get back."

Anger flared in his eyes and his voice was bitter. "Yeah, I guess I knew that." He turned and slammed out of the house.

She slumped against the wall, knowing she'd been a fool, stunned he had left. Nothing, absolutely nothing, was different. His leaving hurt just as much as ever because she loved him just as much as ever.

Blindly, with some vague idea of finding her purse and walking home through the rain, she went into the kitchen. There she found Laura standing white-faced by the sink. She raised frightened eyes.

Forgetting her own troubles, Ginny hurried toward her. "Laura, what's wrong?"

Weakly Laura reached out. "We'd better get to the hospital. I think I'm in labor."

# CHAPTER NINE

"How do you feel?"

"Like something big is about to happen to me," Laura answered dryly, then gasped as another pain hit her. "The baby's not due for another two weeks." Her eyes begged for reassurance.

Ginny gulped and supported her friend as they moved to a kitchen chair. "Everything's going to be fine," she babbled, trying to hide her own terror. Though shaken by the knowledge she was still in love with Bret, had always been in love with him despite what she had tried to tell herself, she now had to concentrate on Laura. "It's just that this kid can't wait to meet his parents." Ginny cast around for the phone, which she spied beside the door to the sun room. "I guess I should ask how far apart the pains are?"

"About five minutes." Laura grimaced. "I've been uncomfortable all day, but didn't realize it was labor. Next time I'll know."

Ginny gaped at her. "You want there to be a next time? You're the most courageous woman I know."

Laura laughed, then groaned.

"Don't worry," Ginny said. "I'll take care of everything." Brave words for someone whose knees were knocking, she thought. "John Clay is your doctor, isn't he?"

Laura nodded and Ginny grabbed the phone to punch out the number she'd known for years. After speaking with him, she called the hospital to tell them Laura was on the way, and then called the fire department so that they could alert Sam and Bret.

She hung up and dashed about locating Laura's coat and suitcase, thankful it had been packed. And as she went, she cursed the Calhoun men for leaving. Though she knew it made little sense, her true irritation was reserved for Bret. He hadn't needed to be at the fire, but his thirst for adventure had simply been too strong to ignore. He hadn't even left her the car!

When she'd bundled Laura into her coat, Ginny helped her down the front steps, now slick with rain, and into Sam's Thunderbird. She rushed back to turn off lights and lock the house, then slid behind the wheel. She quailed for a moment, seeing the array of lights and gadgets facing her. "Great," she muttered, "a rolling Disneyland."

"Don't make me laugh," Laura begged with a breathless giggle, then crumpled in pain.

"I've never driven anything like this before."

Recovering from the contraction, Laura straightened and caught her breath. She smiled ruefully. "It's just like any other car, only dressed up fancier. Did you ever hear about the time I wrecked this car?"

"No." Ginny started the engine, feeling immeasurably cheered that Laura could still make jokes. "You'll have to tell me about it someday when we've got less on our minds." She gave Laura a sly glance. "I dropped a bunk bed on Bret last weekend."

Laura sighed theatrically. "A real Calhoun woman. I knew there was hope for you." Her sigh turned to a gasp. "I think we'd better hurry."

Spurred by necessity, Ginny hit the gas. Before they'd reached the end of the street, the rain had turned to sleet. It fell, cold and dangerous, onto the blacktop before them. Making an effort to calm herself, Ginny moved at a snail's pace, conscious of Laura's every contraction.

They reached the hospital at last and Ginny dashed inside. She was all but dancing with anxiety as she approached the nurse who matter-of-factly took the handles of a nearby wheelchair and rolled it outside for Laura.

Ginny and the nurse helped Laura into the chair just as Laura was gripped with another pain.

"This seems to be moving faster than I expected," Laura panted.

"Consider yourself lucky," the nurse answered. "Most first babies take their sweet time arriving. Yours seems to be in a hurry."

Ginny gave Laura a reassuring hug, whispering again that everything would be fine. With a grateful smile, Laura nodded and the nurse wheeled her away.

Feeling as if she had just run fifty wind sprints, Ginny collapsed into a waiting-room chair and mopped the rain from her face and hair with a handful of tissues. Pulling out a brush, she attempted to make herself presentable, sat for a few moments, then stood to prowl around the room. Although the tables in the room were piled high with outdated magazines Ginny didn't bother grabbing one and trying to read. Her mind was too full of worry for Laura—and for Bret.

At least Laura had competent professionals looking after her and was doing something that had been done for eons. But then, so was Bret, she thought bitterly. He had blithely ridden into danger as men always had, leaving behind the woman who loved him.

Ginny crossed her arms over her stomach and slid down into a chair again. To be fair, Bret didn't know she loved him. And if she had her way he would never find out. She vowed she had cried her last tear over him.

In less than half an hour Sam came in, still dressed in his protective gear. Ginny told Sam what had happened and he rushed off to be with his wife. There was no sign of Bret.

Ginny continued to wait alone, alternately pacing and trying to relax in the chair that seemed to have been designed specifically with discomfort in mind.

Another hour passed before an overjoyed Sam burst back into the waiting room and announced that he and Laura were the parents of a healthy baby boy. He said Laura was doing well and that they were naming him Travis, after Sam and Bret's father.

"Oh, Sam, that's wonderful. Congratulations!" Ginny leapt up, and he danced her wildly around the waiting room, the two of them laughing with relief and happiness. Bret arrived, streaked with dirt and soot, and they whirled to a stop. When Sam told him the news Bret clapped his brother on the back and the two of them shook hands.

Seeing them together reminded Ginny she was only a friend, no longer a part of their family. Quietly she turned to find her jacket and purse.

"I told the nurse that the baby's aunt and uncle would want to see him before they left," Sam said, still giddy and apparently unaware he'd referred to Ginny as his son's aunt. "She said she'd bring him over to the nursery window. Don't expect too much," he warned, though his huge smile gave evidence of his pride. "The kid's the spitting image of that cartoon character, Mr. Magoo."

Sam hurried back to Laura while Bret and Ginny made their way down the hall. As promised, the nurse held up the tiny boy whose pink face clashed with his ginger-colored hair. Ginny forgot her anger with Bret as she leaned eagerly toward the window for a better look.

Once they were finished admiring him, Ginny turned away, planning to leave a message for Sam that she was taking his car home for the night and would return it in the morning.

Bret fell in step beside her. "He's really something, isn't he?"

"Who? The baby? Yes." She smiled. "I was afraid he was going to arrive before we got here, but everything worked out okay. I guess I worry too much."

"Are you admitting that sometimes you worry unnecessarily?"

Ginny shot him a scorching glance and walked faster down the carpeted hallway. "I think that's stretching the point a bit." She stopped at the nurse's station and left the message for Sam, then headed for the door. Bret was right behind her and caught her just before she exited through the wide glass doors.

"Ginny, we need to talk." He took her arm and swung her to face him.

"We've talked." Up until this moment she'd avoided looking at him too closely. Now she could see that soot from the fire had drifted over his face and settled into the faint creases around his eyes. Rain and perspiration had streaked it across his cheeks. Seeing that made her realize how close he must have been to the fire.

To her horror she felt tears welling up in her eyes. She swallowed and faced him, her lips pressed firmly together. She willed her voice not to crack. "I asked you not to go to that fire, but you went, anyway."

"Sam had to come here, and I was the only one who could take his place."

"You didn't know that when you left the house." She stabbed her thumb at her chest. "*I* could have covered that fire. It's my job. You've also got another reporter and a photographer who could have gone." She pulled her arm from his grasp. "You went because you can't live without the excitement. I guess I've known that all along, and you just proved me right. Webster isn't the place for you. Go back to the city."

"This isn't about me. It's about you. You're trying to find an excuse to push me away. I'm getting too close to you, aren't I? Just like last week in that cabin. I had questions but you wouldn't answer them. You're too immature to trust me—or your own feelings."

"That's ridiculous. I'm not going to stand here in a public place and listen to this." Ginny shouldered her way through the door. A blast of cold rain hit her in the face, almost knocking her backward. Gasping with the shock, she pulled her jacket more tightly around her. Despite its protection, she felt shivers starting deep inside her. She didn't know if they were from cold or from reaction.

But Bret wasn't about to let her get away as easily as she'd hoped. "You'll listen if I have to drag you into the middle of the town square. We're not finished talking, Ginny," he growled in her ear. "This isn't over—"

"It was over a long time ago!" She broke away and rushed through the freezing rain to Sam's car. Tumbling inside, she shoved the key into the ignition and started the engine. In a few minutes she had the heater going and blessed warmth filled the interior. Once that was accomplished she glanced up, ready to pull out.

Bret was in his car. The engine was running and the lights were on, cutting through the growing darkness. She knew he was waiting to follow her home. Gratitude and anger battled within her as she left the parking lot of the small county hospital.

Carefully she guided the car onto the icy road and crept home, all the while conscious of Bret's headlights shining reassuringly in her rearview mirror. All she wanted at that moment was to get inside her nice safe home and crawl under her blankets. There she would try to sort out everything that had happened in the past few hours, including the knowledge she still loved Bret and he hadn't really changed.

She had, though. She knew she couldn't go along with his proposal that they date and get to know each other. Her feelings for him were too strong and too confused for her to try something as innocuous as dating! If she could just get home, she could be alone to try to figure out what to do next.

IT WASN'T TO BE. Ginny reached the big Georgian-style house and parked the car safely enough, even managed to get to the door before Bret caught up with her, but when she had stumbled through the back door and reached inside to switch on the kitchen light, nothing happened. Blindly she fumbled her way across the kitchen and bumped into the refrigerator. She pulled the door open, but its light didn't come on, either, so she knew the electricity was off. She voiced a low and unladylike curse and slammed the door shut.

"Tut, tut, tut," Bret said, having followed her into the room. "That's no way to act over a minor inconvenience." He, of course, had thought to get his flashlight out of his glove compartment and was now shining it around the room. It was the same light they'd used the weekend before. Ginny felt a silly pang of longing as she watched its beam slice through the darkness.

"Look." Bret had crossed to the kitchen window and was staring toward the garage apartment, where a light was still burning. "The apartment must be on a separate circuit. Why don't you come there with me until the power is restored?"

"No, thank you." Ginny ran her hands along the drawer pulls, feeling for the one she knew held a flashlight, candles and matches. Once she had her own flashlight in her hand, she felt much more confident. She played the light around the room, even shining it into his set face. "I can see well enough to start a fire in the fireplace, and...and I can sleep in there tonight. I'll be just fine."

"Dammit, Ginny! For once would you stop being stubborn, pigheaded and self-centered?"

*"Self-centered!"*

"Yes. Did you ever think that maybe I need you to listen to me? Really listen, without having your mind already made up and full of righteous indignation?" He came closer and took her arm. "You're coming to the apartment with me. We're going to sit there and let the storm rage—both inside and out."

Appalled, she stared at him. In the glow of the flashlight she could see his determined expression. She opened her mouth to protest, but he placed a gentle hand over her lips.

"Don't bother to say anything until we get there. I've had all I can take from you. I may not be a real fireman, but I do know how to do a fireman's lift, so if necessary, I'll haul you over my shoulder and up those stairs." He stepped back. "Now move!"

Any woman with common sense knows the benefit of a strategic retreat, and Ginny had always been proud of her common sense. She moved. Out the door and up the steps she went, feet firmly planted with each stride, head held at a regal angle. Bret shut the kitchen door and followed.

On the landing, he unlocked the apartment door and held it open for her. Warmth from baseboard heaters immediately wrapped itself around her.

Bret flipped on the lights and she was greeted by the cheerful murals she had helped create.

"Come on in and join the crowd," he invited, gesturing at the painted animals. "These guys don't take up much space, though. They're one-dimensional."

So was her composure. It was all on the surface. Inside she was a bundle of worry and fright. Nevertheless she walked inside and removed her jacket, then sat in the one comfortable easy chair.

Bret took off his own jacket, then looked down at the streaks of soot on his sweater. "I've got to wash up. Why don't you make some coffee?" He disappeared into the small bathroom.

Grateful for something to do, Ginny walked into the kitchen area and started the coffee. It had barely finished brewing before Bret was back, pulling a clean sweatshirt over his head. He accepted the cup she offered. Carrying her own, she went back to the living room. When she tried to retake her seat in the chair he practically growled at her. "Over here." He settled on the camelback sofa and nodded to indicate the cushion beside him.

Nervously she sat where he wanted, sipped the fragrant brew and avoided his gaze.

After several silent minutes he put his cup down on the coffee table, propped his sock-clad feet on it, settled down low on the cushions and gazed at her shrewdly. "How long have you been afraid I was going to die?"

"*What?* How did—?"

"I finally figured it out." His gray eyes were narrow and assessing, the firm line of his jaw set. "You've been afraid of a lot of things ever since we met. I didn't understand it before, but now I know your biggest fear was that I was going to be killed, that I'd leave you alone just like your mother did."

"Why, that's the most ridiculous thing I've ever heard." She reached up to fluff her hair, but her fingers shook.

"Deny it, then." When she didn't answer, he said, "Ginny, look me in the eye and deny it."

She managed to look at him, but she couldn't deny what he had said, and they both knew why. Because it was true. With trembling hands Ginny leaned forward and placed her cup beside his, then sat back, shoulders hunched, and tucked her clasped hands between her knees.

Maybe it was time to get everything out in the open. In a way it would be a relief to talk about the fears she'd never been able to express when they'd been married.

She took a deep breath and expelled it slowly with her words. "I guess I got scared as soon as we got back from our honeymoon."

"Scared?" He turned toward her and rested his hand gently on her shoulder, lending her his strength and giving her reassurance.

"Yes. I was unbelievably naive for my age." She tucked a strand of hair behind her ear. "I thought we could work everything out no matter what it was, but when I saw how successful you were in your career, the same kind of career I had barely begun, I felt inadequate. My internship was much harder than I thought it would be. I had made good grades in my journalism classes, and I was the fourth generation in my family to go into the newspaper business, so I thought it would be easy. It wasn't. When you were off chasing stories, it was even worse. I thought if I'd been a better wife you would have come home nights."

His face softened. "Oh, honey, that had nothing to do with it. I was a jerk to leave you alone. I thought I could have all the benefits of being married without giving up any of my previous life-style. I knew you were upset, but you didn't tell me why. I nearly died of shock when I came home from the hospital and found that note saying you'd left."

Thinking of how that must have hurt him, she cringed. "The coward's way out. I was petrified every time you were gone. I was convinced you were going to be killed. When you were shot, I knew I couldn't take it anymore. I kept remembering what it was like when my mother died." She paused, regaining control over her shaky voice. "So sudden, so devastating. I couldn't go through it again."

Bret sighed and ran the back of his hand across his mouth. "I lost a parent, too. I thought that would bring us closer together. Instead, it drove us apart. Why didn't you stay and tell me how you felt?"

Ginny swallowed, her face pleading. This was the moment she'd dreaded and tried to avoid for so long. "Because I was a failure at marriage, at the career I'd chosen, at . . . everything. So I came home to my father and sister. I knew I was successful taking care of them. That was something I could do well." She paused, afraid to continue, afraid to stop. She had to tell him, though, so she went on, "And I tried my darnedest to fall out of love with you."

"Did you succeed?"

Those three words demanded the truth from her. She lifted her head and met his gaze. "No. I've never stopped loving you. That's why I've fought you so hard since you came to Webster."

His smile was slow in forming and long in lasting. "I've loved you since those first seconds I saw you at Sam's wedding, and I suspect I'll love you until the day I die."

Her eyes closed as tears welled up. "Oh, Bret." There was no more need for words. She reached for him, sliding her hands up and over his shoulders as he clasped her around the waist and drew her close. The joy they felt was matched by the passion that burst between them. Months of denial and need fueled their kiss. There was none of his usual teasing or her usual hesitation. They gave and took equally.

"You were never a failure, Ginny," he whispered against her hair. "You were always perfect, and I was a damned fool not to realize what I had in you. I thought since falling in love was so easy, things would stay easy." He held her away from him. "I began to understand it the night we went to the high-school open house."

"Understand what?" She was smiling happily, amazed she'd been so reluctant to tell him everything.

"I understood how failure affected you—when you told me about having started high school when you were only twelve. You felt guilty because you couldn't handle the situation. I thought, my God, she was barely a kid, and one who had just lost her mother, but you believed you'd failed to live up to people's expectations."

She nodded, giving him a wry smile. "I guess you're right. I never thought of it that way."

"I think you were bothered that you didn't do as good a job of editing the *Herald* as your father had. You saw it as another failure."

"Yes, I did," she admitted.

"Editing isn't your forte, though. But you have done a great job on the school and community-affairs column. And your guest editorials on world affairs was a great idea."

She basked in his praise. It was so wonderful to have someone to share things with. It surprised her to realize that this was what marriage was all about. Sharing was what Sam and Laura had and what she and Bret had missed.

Bret turned her so that she could rest across his lap and gaze into his face. Happily she clasped her fingers together behind his neck.

He kissed her again. "I love you."

She rested her forehead against his solid Calhoun jaw and closed her eyes. For the first time in a year she felt truly at peace. "And I love you." She tilted her head back and watched him with eyes full of teasing humor. "This explains why you came to Webster."

"I wouldn't have come to Webster if not to get you back."

"I thought as much."

"So, where do we go from here?"

She glanced into the far corner, her blue eyes full of sensual promise. "To bed?"

He laughed and rested his forehead against hers. His breathing was ragged. "Oh, Lord, honey, I've been waiting for a long time to hear you say that, but we're not going to do it."

"We're not?"

"Don't sound so appalled. I've always thought of myself as your husband since the day we were married, but I wasn't very good at the job. I let you get away. This time we're going to do everything right."

"Right? How?" She couldn't keep the disappointment out of her voice.

"We're going to have a big church wedding. Your father hated that our first wedding was a courthouse quickie. This time he's going to give you away, and your sister is going to be your maid of honor, and my brother Will can be best man."

She closed her eyes. "Please don't tell me you want Travis to be the ring bearer, or we won't be getting married for five years!"

He chuckled. "No, no. Even I don't have that much stamina. We can work out the rest of the details later. In the meantime why don't you stay the night? I'll hold you, just hold you like I did at the cabin."

"You're crazy."

"Nah, it's a great idea. Besides, you don't want to stay in that big empty house all alone."

Ginny raised herself to grasp handfuls of his thick hair. "You're asking a lot of me, mister."

He howled in mock pain, but his eyes were warm. "I'm only asking for your presence in my bed. In a few weeks, I'll ask for your body. You know, it amazes me that an old divorced lady like you can still blush." He gave her a quick kiss and tumbled her off his lap. "Come on, you can have the bed and I'll sleep here, if you think you can't trust yourself."

She made a face at him that brought a grin to his lips as he pulled open drawers and searched through them. At last he drew out one of his T-shirts and threw it to her. "Your negligee, madam."

With a toss of her head, Ginny flounced into the bathroom. She pushed the door shut and stood hugging herself in pure joy. This was what she wanted, had always wanted, to have Bret back and be sure of his love. Things were going to be wonderful from now on.

She showered eagerly and pulled on the shirt that barely covered the tops of her thighs. She preened in front of the mirror, wondering how strong Bret's resolve was.

When she emerged from the bathroom Bret turned from where he'd been spreading blankets on the couch and whistled appreciatively. He didn't touch her, though, much to her disappointment. "You know, I've always thought you had the most spectacular legs I've ever seen. If you'd been wearing a short dress the day we met, I would have kidnapped you then and there."

She folded her hands behind her back and rocked onto her heels as she gave him a coy glance. "I probably would have let you."

Desire flared in his eyes. He seemed to tamp it down, but his voice sounded strange. "Stop tempting me, woman, and get into bed. We'll start making plans tomorrow. This is going to be a *short* engagement."

Ginny did as he said, slipping between sheets that smelled of his after-shave. She would sleep well knowing he was close by. He sat on the side of the bed to kiss her, telling her once again he loved her, then moved around turning off lights and settling onto his makeshift bed.

Although her mind was full of the day's events and her recaptured love, Ginny fell asleep quickly.

SHE BLINKED HER EYES against the bright sunshine, patting the pillow beside her as usual. This time it wasn't a frustrating dream of Bret that had awakened her, but the telephone. She glanced about for Bret, but couldn't see him or hear the shower running. Finally she grabbed the receiver and dragged it under the blankets. "H'lo?"

"Bret?" the male voice on the other end questioned.

Ginny cleared her throat. "He's not here right now."

"But I'll bet he's been there."

The crack of harsh familiar laughter brought her wide awake. She erupted from beneath the covers. She would know that cynical laugh anywhere. "Frank Brevard? Is that you?" Chills swept through her although the room was warm.

"Sure is, sweetheart. So Bret accomplished his mission? Got you back. Well, it's about damned time. I'm sick of waiting for him to come home. I need him. Got a new assignment all lined up for him just like he wanted. When will you two be getting here?"

# CHAPTER TEN

"HAS THIS ALL BEEN an act?" Ginny asked as soon as Bret walked in the door. She was on her knees in the middle of the bed, the covers clutched to her chin.

He was carrying a bag of doughnuts from Merrick's Bakery. Two weekend newspapers were tucked under his arm.

Warned by her tone and the anger that flashed in her eyes, Bret crossed to the kitchen table and set everything down before answering. "Has what been an act?"

"You had no real interest in living in Webster," she accused, not even trying to disguise her hurt. "You moved here just to get me to come back to you. Why? Because I was the one who got away?"

To her further irritation, Bret took his time removing his jacket and hanging it on the back of a chair. Then he rolled up the sleeves of his plaid flannel shirt. All the while, he regarded her carefully. "Have you developed some kind of brain fever overnight? I thought things were fine when you went to sleep. Did you have a bad dream?"

"Yes. Yes, I have, and I'm only now waking up." She dropped the covers and, moving to the edge of the mattress, slid to the floor. The painted wood was cold against her feet as she marched over to him, but she barely noticed. "Frank Brevard just called."

Bret went very still, his eyes wary. "Did he? What did he say?"

"That he's glad we're back together and he has your next assignment all lined up. Why couldn't you have been honest with me?"

"I've never lied to you."

"Well, you haven't exactly been truthful, either. You're not interested in running a small-town paper. Admit it. When you left Memphis you had no intention of staying in Webster."

"I admit it."

His quiet words took all the fire out of her. Somehow she had entertained the faint hope it wasn't true. She stared at him for a long time, taking in the closed expression on his face. Finally she turned her face away. "I see."

He reached out and tugged at her chin, forcing her to face him. She tried to struggle, but he wouldn't let her go. "When I took the job with your dad I was still damned angry that you'd left me. I was determined to get at the truth about why you'd left. I didn't care a hoot about running a weekly paper in a one-horse town."

"Well, now you know why I left, and now *you* can leave." She waved her hand in an airily careless gesture, but she felt humiliated that she had trusted him enough to reveal her secret fears. She was even more humiliated to think she had believed he loved her. People don't lie to the ones they love.

"I changed my mind, though," Bret said, raising his voice to get her attention. "I knew I needed a change, but I wasn't sure what it should be. Once I was here, I liked it. I liked being near my brother, I liked Webster and I even liked working with you, know-it-all that you were. I finally figured out that this was what I wanted."

"Oh, really?" Her voice was rich with skepticism.

"Yes!" Bret dragged a hand through his hair. "Oh, hell, why am I bothering to tell you this? You've already made up your mind. You'll probably just run away again."

If there was one thing she had learned it was that running away didn't solve anything. The biggest problem had been her doubts about herself, and she'd taken those right along with her.

"Why should I, since you'll be leaving? Heading back to Memphis, your job and all those people who admire you so much?"

"Did you ever ask yourself why your father hired me? Out of all the qualified newspapermen in the world, why me?"

"Because he was fooled into thinking you wanted to make a life in Webster so that you'd be near your family."

"*You* were my family, dammit, and Hugh knew that! He hired me because he wanted us to get back together."

"No!"

They had been standing toe-to-toe, but now Ginny swung away from him. "He knew how you'd hurt me."

"He was playing matchmaker. He called me, said he wanted to retire and offered me the job."

"I don't believe it."

"It's true. He didn't even bother to interview anybody else."

The firmness in his voice convinced her he was telling the truth. But unable to believe that her father would have been such a meddler, she said, "It can't be true."

Bret's hard expression melted fractionally and his voice became gruffly sympathetic. "It is. He said if I hurt you again he'd horsewhip me, but after I took the job I realized I must not have hurt you too much or you would have fought harder against my being hired."

"What do you mean?"

"I mean if you had dug your heels in and refused to work with me, Hugh never would have hired me." Bret stepped closer to her. "Why didn't you dig in your heels, Ginny? Could it be because you wanted me but couldn't admit it even to yourself? Were you glad I came after you so you wouldn't have to admit you'd made a mistake in leaving me and then beg me to take you back?"

"Beg you?" She was so furious she could hardly get the words out. "In a pig's eye! You said yourself that you only came to Webster to get me back."

"And you're insulted by that? I meant I could have found a job anywhere, but this is where I wanted to be. The question is, what did you, and your father, want?"

Ginny smoothed her hair and tucked strands behind her ears. Her blue eyes were troubled as she looked at him. "I can't speak for Dad."

Bret blew out a disgusted breath. "Honey, you can't even speak for yourself. Why don't you ask yourself why you're so upset about this? You can think about it over doughnuts and coffee." His gaze shifted to take in all of her. "While you're at it, why don't you get dressed? It's hard to argue with a woman who's wearing nothing but my T-shirt."

"I'll do better than that. I'll go home and call my father."

"Suit yourself." He shrugged as if he didn't care and began rummaging through the bag he'd brought from the bakery. "You could call from here."

Ginny ignored him, grabbed her things and ducked into the bathroom. She dressed in a hurry, but by the time she was ready, he had coffee made. The inviting aroma permeated the small apartment.

"Sure you don't want to stay?" he asked, gesturing with the doughnut in his hand.

"No, thanks." She opened the door and left. He followed her.

"Got some heavy-duty thinking to do? Well, find out what your father's motives were in hiring me, then ask yourself what your motives were in letting him. And then ask yourself why you're reacting like this to Frank's call. Remember, *he's* the one who said he had an assignment ready for me. I never said I'd take it. Are you just scared? Are you realizing that you're going to have to accept me the way I am? That if we get remarried this time it's for keeps? I won't let you go again."

Ginny gave him an exasperated look and hurried to the house. In a way he was right. She did have some serious thinking to do. She'd been in Bret's company almost exclusively for the past week, and she needed some distance.

The electricity had come on during the night, so the house was warm. Ginny headed straight for the telephone to call Hugh.

She paused with her hand on the receiver. No. This was the kind of thing that should be talked about in person. She changed into fresh jeans and a bulky pink sweater, then rushed out to her car. As she was driving away she saw Bret standing at the top of the stairs to his apartment, but she kept going.

Once she had completed the hour's drive on the highway and turned onto the dirt road, it was easy for her to find her way to the cabin Hugh had rented. The road hadn't been improved by a week of intermittent rain, which meant she had to be careful to keep the car from skidding into the mud. When she passed the place where she and Bret had spent the night she deliberately kept her eyes focused on the road.

Hugh's cabin looked cozy in the morning mist, with smoke curling from the chimney and lights in the windows. He came out onto the porch when he heard her drive up. He was dressed in an old sweater with patches on the elbows and a pair of gray flannel slacks.

He was waiting at the bottom of the steps when she stopped the car.

"Hi, Ginny girl. I didn't expect to see you for a while." He caught the determined light in her eyes. "What's wrong?"

She slammed the car door and stalked over to him as she blurted out her question.

"Dad, why did you hire Bret?"

He had been reaching out to hug her, but now he drew back. "Whoa, what's this all about? I thought things were going okay."

"Did you hire him so that we'd get back together?"

"Now, honey," he wheedled, "why don't we go inside?" He climbed the steps and swung open the door.

Since he was holding it for her she could hardly refuse, but she pressed him for an answer as soon as they were in the cabin. "Did you?"

He pursed his lips and shifted his gaze away from her. "Oh, all right. Yes, I did. I couldn't stand to see you moping around. I knew you needed him."

Her knees gave way. Ginny slumped into a chair beside the kitchen table and rested her forehead in her palm. "But, Dad, you didn't like Bret when I married him."

He gaped at her for a moment, then said, "Now wait a minute, missy. I liked him fine. I just thought you married him too quickly. When you came home I saw that you still loved him no matter what crazy stories you told yourself, but you were too stubborn to go back and work things out. Hiring him was the only way I could think of to get you two together. I was pretty amazed he even listened to my offer."

"He had reasons of his own."

"So, what's wrong with that?" Hugh sat down next to her, taking her hand in his. "What's the matter with having a man love you so much he's willing to quit his job and follow you?"

"Nothing...I guess. I just feel manipulated. By him—" she looked up accusingly "—and by you."

Hugh had the grace to blush. "It was all for a good cause, though."

"You weren't really having a relapse, were you?"

"Uh, no. I was completely recovered months ago, but I knew I could get you to do what I wanted without an argument if I pretended to be sick. I, uh, faked the cough."

"I should have known, especially when you refused to call Dr. Clay." She was still upset with him, but genuinely curious now. "How did you make your face turn red like that?"

He beamed. "It was easy. I saw Jimmy Blaines do it one day when he was trying to convince Margie he was too sick to go to school. He showed me how." Hugh's face took on a miffed expression. "The only problem was that the little hustler kept demanding more money."

Ginny stared at him. "Good grief, a ten-year-old blackmailer?"

"Afraid so."

She was just thinking of a whole new set of questions when she heard another car outside. Ginny recognized the sound of the engine even before they looked out to see Bret's car.

"Why did I bother to move out here?" Hugh grumbled. "I should have rented space in the middle of the Webster town square."

"You should have been honest with me," Ginny said sweetly, and watched as he went to open the door for Bret.

Bret entered cautiously. "Had all your questions answered yet?"

"Not all of them." Her voice was stiff, but she was beginning to feel better than when she'd arrived. "Dad was just confessing that he faked his cough so I'd go along with his plans to hire you."

"I thought as much." Bret glanced around as he removed his coat. "Got any coffee, Hugh? My breakfast was interrupted. I had to follow my hot-headed fiancée. I was afraid she'd drive off into a muddy ditch or have car trouble on the way down here. Radiator hoses have a tendency to break in this vicinity."

Hugh paused as he was reaching for the pot. "No kidding?"

"You wouldn't know anything about that, would you?"

Ginny sat up straight and looked from Hugh to Bret as understanding hit her. "Oh, Dad, you didn't."

He shrugged sheepishly. "It seemed like a good idea at the time. How was I supposed to know you'd lock the keys in the car and nearly freeze to death before you found someplace to spend the night?"

"That's what you were doing while Bret and I were in the kitchen, wasn't it?" Ginny accused. "That wasn't mud on your hands. It was car grease."

"Oh, all right, all right. I admit I cut the radiator hose so that it would break a little ways down the road. I wanted to force you two to spend time alone together and start working things out. That's why I moved out here in the first place. I figured if you didn't have to worry about me, Ginny, Bret would have a clear field."

She clapped her hands onto her hips. "You make me sound like the prize at the end of a race."

Hugh's grin was unrepentant. "Did it work?"

"Not quite the way you planned," Bret said, sipping his coffee. His eyes held a hint of laughter as he watched Ginny. "But given time, things might turn out just fine."

Hugh stood suddenly. "I think I'll go for a walk."

Ginny nearly choked. "Not another one!"

"I'll just walk," he promised, bustling around hunting for his jacket. "No more monkey business. I think you two can handle things from here on out."

"Thanks for the vote of confidence," she muttered as he hurried outside, slamming the door behind him.

For several seconds there was silence in the room, broken only by the tick of the clock over the mantel and the crackle of burning wood in the fireplace. At last Bret cleared his throat.

"So, where are we on your list of complaints about me?"

Put that way, it sounded as if she was being silly. Maybe she was. Bret might have been right when he said she was scared. Ginny put her head in her hands. "I...I don't know."

"Ginny, believe me, I never told Frank that I'd come back. He was fishing, hoping I'd change my mind. Since I received the MacKellar he's been hounding me to work for him. But that's not what I want anymore. I like living in Webster. I like being my own boss. In fact, your dad's been talking about selling the paper to me."

Ginny knew she should have been outraged, but so much had happened in the past twelve hours she was beyond worrying about ownership of the paper.

He seemed to understand, anyway. "Maybe I should say, sell it to *us*." He put his coffee mug down and came around the table. "How about it? Shall we get married, run a newspaper and raise babies?"

Ginny didn't answer right away. Instead, she shoved up the sleeves of her sweater, then nervously ran her hand over her hair. When she finally spoke it was in a whisper. "What if our marriage fails again?"

Bret reached down to wrap his hands around her upper arms and lift her to her feet. "It won't. Whatever problems we have we can solve together. You've seen the kind of marriage Sam and Laura have. You think they don't have problems? Sure, they do, but they work them out. We can work ours out." He laughed helplessly, "Besides, what more could possibly happen?"

She smiled, but it was a wryly mocking one.

"Well, let me rephrase that. What could possibly happen as long as your father doesn't meddle?" When she didn't answer he said, "I quit my job to come after you and let you dunk me in a tank full of cold water, strand us in the middle of nowhere, break a bunk bed over my body... What more do I have to do to prove I love you?"

What, indeed? All her concerns disappeared. She was a different woman than she had been a year ago, and he was a different man. She looked up into his anxious face with eyes full of love. "Nothing," she said, reaching up to twine her arms around his neck. "Absolutely nothing at all."

Relief replaced the anxiety in his eyes, and Bret pulled her close to kiss her lovingly. "There is one more thing I want to ask you."

Dreamily she kissed his jaw, rough with the beard he hadn't had time to shave off that morning. "Anything."

"This time, will you take my name? Or at least hyphenate it? I want us to be real partners."

"McCoy-Calhoun? Calhoun-McCoy? I don't think so. It's too much of a mouthful." She grinned impishly. "Laura called me a real Calhoun woman. Maybe it's time I took the name, too."

"Whatever you want, honey," he breathed against her lips. "Just so you're my real wife and don't ever leave me again."

# EPILOGUE

"A Christmastime wedding was a perfect idea, Ginny," Doris said, her eyes tearing up as she fussed with Ginny's airy tulle veil. It fell away from a headpiece of blue satin roses and tiny silver stars, making Ginny's hair and shoulders look as if they were sprinkled with light.

"I'm amazed you pulled it all together in less than two months," Carrie added.

"Bret said he wouldn't stand for a long engagement." Ginny turned before the mirror to give Carrie, Doris and Laura a better view of her outfit, as well as to get one for herself. "Asking you to make my dress was the perfect idea," Ginny said, awed by the fabulous design Doris had created.

Even though she was marrying the same man, it *was* a second marriage, and Ginny had decided to follow tradition by being wed in a colored gown. Doris had found silk *peau de soie* in the palest imaginable shade of blue, covered the skirt with lace woven from silver thread and made a gown that seemed to shimmer whenever Ginny moved.

The bodice was plain, with a wide fichu collar that set off Ginny's lovely face and shoulders. The sleeves of lace matched the overskirt. Her bouquet, still nestled in the florist's box, was of white roses and blue orchids.

"If I'd had a daughter of my own I would have wanted to make her wedding dress." After a few final adjustments Doris stepped back. "There now. You look beautiful. I can't tell you how disappointed I was when you didn't let me have this pleasure the first time around." She turned and shook a finger at Carrie. "Don't you go getting any ideas about eloping."

Carrie held up her hands in protest. "Don't worry. I won't be getting married for a long time. I want a career. Besides, you and Ginny are making up for what you missed before. Bret says nothing's been done at the *Herald* office in a month because you two have had your heads together over wedding plans."

Ginny laughed. "He was in on the plans, too, so he'd better stop complaining."

She looked around at her sister and friends. Doris had a new suit of Christmas green that complemented her bright hair, dyed red for the occasion. She even had a piece of holly pinned among her curls.

Carrie and Laura, Ginny's attendants, wore matching gowns of midnight-blue crushed velvet. Their dresses had gently draped skirts that reached the floor and moiré satin bows that cinched their waists. The bodices were covered in white Irish lace, and their bouquets were white roses tied with silver ribbon.

"I'm glad little Travis got over his sniffles so you could be in my wedding," Ginny said to Laura.

"I threatened him," Laura admitted. "I told him I'd present him with a baby brother next year if he didn't get well. Can you imagine another Calhoun man in the house? I'd never survive." Her shudder of distaste was belied by the happy glow on her face.

Ginny shook her head. "The mind boggles." She sighed with satisfaction. "But you never know. Bret and I may have a little Calhoun by this time next year.''

"You will if Bret has anything to say about it,'' Carrie assured her. She smiled as she recognized the notes of the hymn that was to precede the processional. "That's our cue. Are you ready?''

Ginny picked up her bouquet and turned it so the silver ribbons fluttered against the front of her skirt. "More than you'll ever know.'' She alternately felt sheer happiness and sheer anxiety, although she no longer worried that she and Bret couldn't make a second marriage work. This time they both knew exactly what they wanted—each other and nothing else.

They were even going on a real honeymoon, and while they were gone, Hugh would run the *Herald*. When they returned they'd live in her family home. Hugh planned to stay in the cabin in the woods and finish his book, then live in the garage apartment if he didn't find himself a smaller home.

Laura and Carrie led the way out of the small room they'd been using. Hugh was waiting in the foyer, tugging at his blue cummerbund. For weeks he'd been insufferably smug and self-important about having pulled the whole courtship and ceremony off.

In spite of that, or maybe because of it, Ginny adored him. She took his arm and squeezed it, then stood on tiptoe to catch a glimpse of Bret standing at the front of the church, tall and handsome in his gray tuxedo. His gaze seemed to sharpen when he saw her. The intensity of his look reminded her of the day they'd met. Warmth flooded through her and her nervousness eased a bit. Whatever happened, she knew she didn't have to be concerned about the future. It was secure as long as she had his love.

A thought struck her just as the organist sounded the first notes of Lohengrin's "Wedding March." Ginny leaned forward to whisper urgently in her sister's ear. "Carrie, you've met Bret and Sam's brother, Will, haven't you?"

Carrie blinked uncertainly. "Sure, last night at the rehearsal. Why?"

"Just a warning. Something strange seems to happen to the Calhoun men at weddings."

Carrie rolled her eyes. "Not with me, it won't. After all the problems you and Laura have had with these guys? Uh-uh. Not me."

Ginny winked at Laura, then fluttered her fingers at her sister to get her started down the aisle. Right on the beat, Carrie stepped forward and Laura followed.

Hugh tightened his grip on Ginny's arm. "Well, Ginny girl, I think you're doing the right thing."

She looked down the long carpeted aisle, past the pews decorated with evergreen boughs tied with blue and silver ribbon to the man who waited for her. He smiled back at her as if the two of them shared a wonderful secret. "I know I am, Dad. I know I am."

**Where do you find hot Texas nights, smooth Texas charm, and dangerously sexy cowboys?**

## *Crystal Creek*

### WHITE LIGHTNING

### by Sharon Brondos

**Back a winner—Texas style!**

Lynn McKinney knows Lightning is a winner and she is totally committed to his training, despite her feud with her investors. All she needs is time to prove she's right. But once business partner Dr. Sam Townsend arrives on the scene, Lynn realizes time is about to run out!

CRYSTAL CREEK reverberates with the exciting rhythm of Texas. Each story features the rugged individuals who live and love in the Lone Star State. And each one ends with the same invitation...

### Y'ALL COME BACK...REAL SOON!

**Don't miss WHITE LIGHTNING by Sharon Brondos. Available in June wherever Harlequin books are sold.**

---

**Harlequin is proud to present our best authors and their best books. Always the best for your reading pleasure!**

Throughout 1993, Harlequin will bring you exciting books by some of the top names in contemporary romance!

In June, look for *Threats and Promises* by

BARBARA DELINSKY

The plan was to make her nervous....

Lauren Stevens was so preoccupied with her new looks and her new business that she really didn't notice a pattern to the peculiar "little incidents"—incidents that could eventually take her life. However, she did notice the sudden appearance of the attractive and interesting Matt Kruger who *claimed* to be a close friend of her dead brother....

**Find out more in THREATS AND PROMISES ... available wherever Harlequin books are sold.**

BOB2

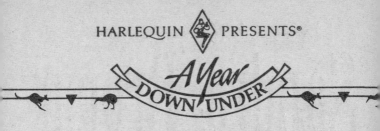

HARLEQUIN PRESENTS®

*A Year* DOWN UNDER

In 1993, Harlequin Presents celebrates the land down under. In June, let us take you to the Australian Outback, in OUTBACK MAN by Miranda Lee, Harlequin Presents #1562.

Surviving a plane crash in the Australian Outback is surely enough trauma to endure. So why does Adrianna have to be rescued by Bryce McLean, a man so gorgeous that he turns all her cherished beliefs upside-down? But the desert proves to be an intimate and seductive setting and suddenly Adrianna's only realities are the red-hot dust *and* Bryce....

Share the adventure—and the romance— of A Year Down Under!

Available this month in
A YEAR DOWN UNDER

SECRET ADMIRER
by Susan Napier
Harlequin Presents #1554
Wherever Harlequin books are sold.

HARLEQUIN ROMANCE®

Let Harlequin Romance® take you

# BACK TO THE

*Come to* the Kincaid Ranch, near Red Horse, Wyoming.

*Meet* rancher Ethan Kincaid and a woman named Maggie Deaton—ex-rancher and ex-convict!

*Read* THE BAD PENNY by Susan Fox—her first Harlequin Romance in 4 years! Available in June 1993 wherever Harlequin books are sold.